Other

Marlin

Road Games and Other Weird Tales

The Attic Piranhas

Ravenwood Stepson of Mystery
in
Trumpet of Triton

Copyright © 2019 Marlin Williams

All rights reserved. No part of this book may be reproduced or transmitted in any form or by electronic or mechanical means, including photocopying, recording or by any information storage and retrieval system, without the written permission of the author.

This is a work of fiction. Names, characters, places, and incidents are the product of the author's imagination. Any resemblance to actual person, living or dead, business establishments, event, or locales is entirely coincidental.

Book Cover Design by SelfPubBookCovers.com/ Viergacht

A special thanks to my good friend, Terry Ludwig, for all your help

And the army of Atlantis carried forth with them into battle the Trumpet of Triton. A conch shell, that when blown, possessed the power to drive their enemy deep into madness and reduce whole cities to rubble.

Time: 1936
Place: Manhattan

Old buildings liked to chatter, especially at night, and in the night watchman's twenty-five years of experience, he'd discovered that each one spoke a language of its own.

This was different.

A hum resonated from beneath his feet and sent a shiver down his spine. He'd just completed his rounds upstairs and knew there was nothing inside the building but a bunch of old, dusty relics. But, he hadn't checked the basement where the vault held the museum's most precious valuables. He stood at the mouth of the stairwell leading down into the darkness.

Over the incessant droning, he could hear someone or something moving about. He laid a hand on the nightstick attached to his belt. The security agency that he worked for didn't furnish him with a handgun, and until now, he hadn't cared. Who expected any trouble at a museum?

What he needed was light. In mere seconds, the place could be filled with the magic of electric illumination and put an end to the mystery, but the switch for the light was on the wall at the bottom of the stairs. *Why not place it at the top of the stairs where it made more sense*, he'd often wondered. Now, if someone happened to be down there, the inconvenience was compounded by danger. He pulled the flashlight from its clip and shined it down. It barely lit the throat of the deep stairwell. He silently cursed. To conceal his mission, he extinguished his light.

The hard soles of his shoes telegraphed his descent, and he regretted his last minute decision to substitute loafers for his usual Hush Puppies. He decided to abandon caution and made a clattering dash down the wooden steps and hastily groped the wall for the brass switch, found the knob, and gave it a twist. It clicked. Immediately, the room filled with light.

The pitch of the hum changed, lower, pulsating.

Instantly, the bulbs dangling from the ceiling simultaneously burst.

His heart began to race, and despite feeling dizzy, he called out, "I'm armed!" Light blazed from his flashlight as he flicked it back on and pulled his nightstick. He held it in a death grip above his head and wagged his torch around in an effort to get a bead on the perpetrator. Now, the building shook, from the main floor above, the sound of breaking glass traveled down the stairs. Suddenly, the intruder was revealed in the disc of light. A pair of green glowing eyes stared back.

The next day

Ravenwood cruised his roadster along the city streets feeling gratified by the evening's outcome. He had garnered an invitation to a séance where a clairvoyant, well-known among high society, claimed to conjure up dearly departed loved ones for a hefty fee. Several of her clients were personal friends of his, and he had become suspicious and believed they were being taken by a charlatan. Tonight, his hunch had proven right. Madam Bouvier's spirits were no more than props manipulated by wires and mirrors under the cloak of darkness.

He pulled up to Sussex Towers. A few stars sparkled in the sky and a full moon rose behind the silhouetted buildings across the street. He parked his coupe, deposited his keys in his pocket, and with walking stick in hand, briskly scaled the stone steps to the entrance.

The doorman tipped his hat and opened the door. "Good evening, sir. I hope that you had a pleasant outing."

"Thank you, James, I did." Ravenwood laid a gloved hand on the doorman's shoulder in passing.

Whistling *Pennies from Heaven* he strolled across the grand foyer to the elevator where he ended his warbling concerto and boarded the elegant car.

Over the years, Ravenwood had gotten to know the operator through brief conversations they'd shared on the way to the penthouse. "Evening, Porter."

"Evening, sir." The mesh door swished closed and the car clanked and rattled toward the top. This evening, Porter was quiet. Edgy. Something was amiss. Ravenwood left it alone and they rode in silence.

When he departed the elevator, his uneasiness trailed him along the hallway. He entered his penthouse, and Sterling, his manservant, was not there to greet him and he could sense an unfamiliar presence. Unable to detect whether the person was malevolent or benign, as a precaution, he pulled his custom made Luger from inside his jacket.

Sterling entered the foyer. "I don't think you'll be needing that." He acknowledged the gun with a nod. "She doesn't appear to be dangerous."

"She?"

"There is a Miss Darla Whitfield here to see you, sir."

The name didn't ring a bell. "How did she get up here?" The elevator operator, flashed through his mind. "Never mind—I think I know." Porter was a sucker for women, especially the pretty ones. But one day it could cost him his job—or worse. As Ravenwood shoved the gun back into its holster, he wrinkled his brow. "Did she state her business?"

"I'm afraid she didn't." Sterling took his master's walking stick. After placing it on the console table, he took his coat. "My speculation is that she's here to solicit you for a sizable charitable donation." He hung the jacket on the hall tree. "I tried to discourage her from waiting here for you, but she was quite insistent."

"Where is she now?"

"I had her wait in your library, sir."

Ravenwood didn't want to deal with such a mundane matter, not now. The deadline for his new book on the occult was quickly approaching and he was running behind. "Tell her to schedule a meeting for next week."

"Next week will be too late." The voice was female. A blue-eyed, raven-haired beauty appeared in the living room doorway and entered the foyer. She looked troubled. "I only need a few moments of your time."

"I'm sorry, Miss Whitfield," said Sterling.

"Please." Her eyes implored Ravenwood.

"Master Ravenwood will call you at his earliest convenience." Sterling took a step forward to show her out.

Ravenwood clamped his hand down on the manservant's shoulder and seized him in midstride. "It's all right, Sterling." He turned to the woman. "Let's return to the library." He led the way.

With a look of disapproval on his face, the servant watched as Ravenwood escorted her from the foyer.

Ravenwood stood next to the door and motioned her inside. As she breezed by, he could smell her perfume. Chanel No. 5, if he wasn't mistaken. He rarely was. He followed her in and noticed the valise sitting beside the plush settee. His curiosity grew.

She caught him looking. "I was planning a trip."

Was? He shifted his gaze back to her blue eyes. "Change of plans?"

Her reply was weak. "Yes."

"Please have a seat, Miss Whitfield." He motioned to the settee.

She sat, and when she crossed her legs, the move hiked the hem of her skirt just above the knees.

An alarm sounded in his head. A ploy, no doubt, to soften him up, he thought. It wouldn't be the first time a troubled young woman, in dire straits, sought funds to escape a precarious predicament. He was guessing, but in the meantime, he enjoyed the view of her shapely calves.

"I must apologize for interrupting your evening." She looked nervous and hesitated. "So, I guess I should just state my business." She took a deep breath. "I came to ask for —"

"Money?" He cocked his head.

She looked offended. "No! It's quite another matter entirely."

He missed that one by a mile. Ravenwood suddenly felt embarrassed for his presumptuous interjection. "I'm sorry, Miss Whitfield, it was foolhardy on my part to assume why you're here. So, how can I be of service to you?"

She stared into his eyes as if to read his seriousness. Her reticence was clear.

"Could I interest you in a martini?" he asked, hoping that a drink would ease her tension and loosen her tongue.

She nodded.

"Good." He walked behind the bar to prepare the concoction. "Because I happen to make the best martini in Manhattan." After adding a splash of vermouth and a gentle stir with the glass stick, he held the drink up. "Now, for the most important part." The olive made a splash when he dropped it into the mixture. He walked it over to her. After she took it, Ravenwood sat down next to her.

"Odd," she said.

"What's odd?"

"I could have sworn your eyes were gray." She leaned in for a closer look. "But they're actually blue."

He shrugged. "Must be a trick of the light."

She suddenly became aware that her nose was only inches from his. Her cheeks flared red, and she quickly pulled away. "I'm sorry. I didn't mean to be so forward."

He waved off the incident. "So, let's get back to why you are here."

"Yes. Let's do that." She took a deep breath and spoke quickly. "I've heard that you dabble in cases that deal with the occult."

Dabble? What an understatement. He usually plunged headlong into cases that involved the paranormal. His calm voice belied his piqued curiosity as he answered, "Yes, I suppose I do." He raised a brow. "So, what is this about?"

She took a sip from the martini glass. "A conch shell."

A sea shell? That's all? His interest deflated. Ravenwood had his own pressing affairs to attend. He glanced at his Rolex. The deadline for his book weighed upon him again. He kept his impatience contained as she pressed the crystal rim to her full lips and drank the remaining liquid. When she'd finished, she placed the glass at her feet. She took a deep breath and said, "The conch is the Trumpet of Triton."

Ravenwood gaped, but only momentarily, before his rational logic reined in his exhilaration. He was familiar with the conch shell of mythology. It had been given as a gift to the ruler of Atlantis by the demigod, Triton, to be used against their enemies. When blown, the sound of the horn drove their foe mad and reduced their mighty cities to rubble. Ironically, the written lore claimed it was the power of the trumpet that had sent the great city of Atlantis to the bottom of the ocean after the ruler of Atlantis had denounced his allegiance to Triton. "Is this in jest?" he asked, not bothering to hide his skepticism. "You must be aware that Triton is no more than a mythical character, and the trumpet, a figment of an author's creation."

She stood. There was fire in her eyes. "I can assure you that the Trumpet is real!" She stalked to the window and stared out.

He followed her over and stood at her back. "Have you seen the trumpet?"

She turned and faced him. "No."

"I'm sorry, Miss Whitfield, based on what you've told me I'm afraid I can't be of service to you." He started for the door to dismiss her.

"Wait, please?"

He paused.

"It was stolen and I'm afraid that it has fallen into the wrong hands." The expression on her face validated her concern.

"So, you know who took it."

She nodded.

"Who?"

"If you will accompany me back to the museum, my father can tell you more about it."

Curious, he raised a brow. "Who is your father?"

"Professor Edmond Whitfield. He's the curator at the Davis Museum."

Ravenwood knew the place. It was one of the smaller institutions outside Manhattan. It held some of the rarest and strangest artifacts from around the world. From what he'd heard, many of the objects fell into the realm of questionable authenticity. He shook his head. "I'm afraid that I can't."

"I have proof of the trumpet's power." Sincerity registered on her face.

"What kind of proof?"

"You'll have to see it with your own eyes. Come back with me to the museum and I'll show you."

It seemed that Porter wasn't the only one that was a sucker for a beautiful woman. It would only cost him the evening. "Of course, Miss Whitfield."

She looked relieved "Oh, and one more thing," she said softly.

He watched as she reached down and unfastened the top button of her blouse.

"This is the only way that I can pay you for your services."

Now, Ravenwood was more than intrigued, he was mesmerized as she unfastened the second button.

She dipped her hand into her shirt and dredged up an amulet suspended by a gold chain. "Do you know what this is?"

His discombobulated brain was still trying to fathom what was going on.

"Mister Ravenwood?"

He looked up. "What?"

"This." She jiggled the amulet. "Do you know what this is?"

The spell was broken. He quickly sobered and leaned in for a closer look where the scent of perfume was stronger. It was not the run of the mill gemstone. He nodded. "It's a black diamond."

"It's twenty karats. Would you consider it as payment for your services?" Sterling barged in. The manservant's eyes suddenly widened with surprise as his gaze locked on her open blouse and his master's face inches from her breasts. She and Ravenwood parted like two, passionate, teen-aged lovers caught in the act.

"I'm sorry, sir. I didn't realize that you and the lady were—"

She let the diamond plunge back down to nestle in her bosom.

"What is it, Sterling?" He felt annoyed with the unannounced intrusion.

"I am sorry, sir, but dinner is growing cold."

"Place it in the warmer."

Sterling looked peeved. "But, sir, Beef Wellington is best served hot."

"I'll dine later," answered Ravenwood, his voice stern. "I'm driving Miss Whitfield home." He picked up her bag.

Sterling pressed his lips together and glared at her. "Very well, sir."

Ravenwood took notice of the infraction, but was well aware of Sterling's conventional habit of dining precisely on time each evening. Ravenwood usually conformed easily to his servant's idiosyncrasies, but tonight there was another matter to attend. On his way out of the apartment, he grabbed his gloves, topped his brown locks with a fedora, and grabbed his walking stick. It was carved by the monks of Tibet and housed an epee, a sharp pointed dueling sword.

When they arrived at the elevator, he pressed the button and the cab came clanking up the shaft. The car appeared through the grated gates, came to a stop, and the operator parted the doors. Ravenwood expected to see Porter. Instead, a larger man, wearing an operator's jacket and hat, stood in his place.

The man's deep-set, blue eyes settled on Miss Whitfield and instantly narrowed.

She shrank back and gasped.

Ravenwood's muscles coiled tight. "Who are you, and where's Porter?"

The operator slammed the grated gates shut and pulled the lever back. The cab began to descend and slowly sank from sight.

"You recognized him?" he asked.

She nodded. "He's one of the men threatening my father."

The fine hairs on the nape of Ravenwood's neck bristled. "Let's take the stairs."

They hurried down the twenty flights and were there to meet the elevator in the lobby. When it arrived, the cab was empty.

"How?" she asked.

He shrugged. The only explanation was that the man had gotten off on one of the other floors and sent the elevator down on its own. He could still be in the building, or he could have taken the fire escape down and was out on the street. Ravenwood scooted them through the lobby to the double glass doors.

"Ravenwood, I'm frightened. What if he's out here waiting for us." She latched on to his arm.

"I promise that I won't let anything happen to you." A promise he intended to keep. "Let's go." The doorman was not at his post, so Ravenwood pushed open the door and they stepped out onto the landing. A white, work-truck, with BOROUGH OF MANHATTAN stenciled on the side, blocked one of the lanes. In front of it, a barricade of metal stands and wood planks encompassed an open manhole. He scanned the pedestrians clogging the sidewalk. The man was nowhere in sight.

Suddenly, a strange droning filled the air. It sounded like a kid blowing across the lip of an empty soda bottle, only much louder.

"What is that?" She was still clinging to his arm.

He shook his head, then something caught his eye. He squinted, trying to make out more detail.

She caught him staring "What do you see?"

He pointed a finger at the metal lid next to the open manhole. It quivered and began to dance around.

"What the—" she exclaimed.

The pitch of the drone abruptly changed and increased to ear-splitting decibels. The ground beneath their feet trembled.

Darla placed a hand on her forehead. "I feel faint."

The inside of Ravenwood's head rollicked. He began to feel queasy. Things began to spin. He heard the tinkle of glass raining down on the sidewalk. The buildings began to sway. "We have to get out of here now!" He fought to maintain balance as he rushed her down the steps to his car. Pieces of brick pelted down onto the sidewalk and street. Panicked inhabitants poured out the narrow doors like ants.

"How?" Her eyes were focused on the idle traffic as people abandoned their vehicles and fled.

"I know a way." He opened the passenger door and tossed her bag inside. She tumbled into the seat.

Darla sat rigid, squeezed the lids of her eyes shut, and clapped her hands over her ears. "Please hurry."

As the loud hum continued, he started the car and nosed his roadster into the alley where chunks of building facade littered the path and more was coming down. Ravenwood quickly navigated the narrow passage, jetted out onto the cross street, and floored the accelerator. He watched the unfolding chaos through his rearview mirror while reassuring himself that if they had remained behind, he and Miss Whitfield may have become casualties. Now, out of range of the hum, his clouded mind cleared, and he barreled through the streets darkened as a result of the quake.

With the threat now gone, Miss Whitfield uncovered her ears and slumped back in her seat.

"Are you all right?"

She opened her eyes and turned her head toward him. "I think so, but—" She was staring at him.

"What's the matter?"

"Your eyes."

He adjusted the rearview. The impoverished glow of the full moon provided enough light for Ravenwood to see that his eyes were bloodshot.

She reached up and yanked the mirror. "My God!" She'd been afflicted in the same way.

"That wasn't an ordinary earthquake."

"I know, it wasn't. Now, you must believe me," she replied.

"Are you claiming this has something to do with the Trumpet of Triton?"

She nodded. "Yes."

They both fell silent and Ravenwood spent the time wondering if her story was quickly turning into some bizarre reality. In the past, the supernatural elements of his cases usually turned out to be nothing more than a masterminded deception. It remained to be seen that if it would hold true in this case.

Darla spent the rest of the ride huddled against him.

They arrived. He stopped in front of the massive gothic building, grabbed his walking stick, her valise, and hopped out. Keeping a watchful eye on his surroundings, he rounded the front bumper and opened her door. Still shaky, she got out. Ravenwood held her elbow in support as they climbed the stairs. He looked up at the darkened building. "Are you sure your father is here?"

As her trembling hand worked the key in the lock, she replied, "Yes. He's working late." She peered through the thick glass of the massive wooden door before she shoved it open.

Exercising caution, he followed her in and peered into the dark abyss.

She left his side and felt along the wall for the switch.

He heard it click. The room remained dark-filled.

"There's an electric lantern behind the desk," she said.

He heard the gritty sound of the soles of her shoes scraping the floor as she shuffled toward the desk. A moment later the glow of the filament chased the shadows back. Even though the light was inadequate to brighten the room, it exposed enough detail for Ravenwood to see that most of the overhead lighting were shattered like broken eggshells. "Tonight's quake must have damaged the museum as well." It puzzled him when she shook her head.

"This happened two nights ago."

Strange. Why hadn't he heard about it? Seismic activity of this magnitude would have affected surrounding areas with tremors, and to his knowledge, none had been reported, but the damage to the building was evident. "Were you here when it happened?"

She shook her head. "My father and I were at home. The night watchman called to tell us a terrible sound had ripped through the building and shattered almost all the glass. Of course we drove here immediately."

"What time did this happen?"

"Around midnight."

"Did you report it?"

"No."

A deep, guttural growl penetrated the darkness. From the shadows, two eyes tossed back the muted light as small glowing discs of green. Instinctively, Ravenwood stepped around her and pulled the sword from his walking stick.

"What are you doing?" She stepped in front of him and pushed the blade aside.

The sound of long toenails clacked out a repetitive rhythm on the hardwood floor as a form untangled from the shadows and cautiously moved closer. The figure was squat and walked on all fours. It was only a dog. He suddenly felt foolish and returned the razor-edged steel to the walking stick.

The border collie stopped within feet of them and growled.

"Jake, come here, boy." Immediately, the dog wagged its tail and padded slowly toward his mistress. She scratched the dog behind the ears while looking up at Ravenwood. "His behavior has been strange since the night of the quake."

"So Jake was here that night?"

"Yes. We had left him here with the night watchman to help guard the place."

The dog growled at Ravenwood again.

Her full lips were now close to the dog's ear as she spoke. "Mister Ravenwood is our friend." The collie parted from her and nudged his hand. "That's a good boy," she said.

He gave the dog a scratch behind the ears. "Does Jake run the place?"

"Most of the time." She managed a laugh.

He sensed hidden eyes watching him. A man made invisible by the dark. Ravenwood peered into the gloom around them, searching the voyeur out.

The wash of a flashlight flowing down the stairs broke his psychic connection. An elderly gentleman was clad in rumpled clothes and held a handgun in one hand and a flashlight in the other. "Who's there?" He shined the light in their faces.

Jake began to whine and wagged his tail.

"Father, it's me."

He lowered the light to their feet. "What are you doing here?" He looked both surprised and angry as he nervously tucked the gun into the pocket of his slacks. "I could have mistaken you for an intruder!" A swatch of white hair hung over his wrinkled brow as he looked down and checked the time on his pocket watch. "You should be at the train station by now."

"I've decided not to leave."

He looked alarmed. "You must!" He trundled down the remaining stairs. "It's much too dangerous for you to remain here." He looked at Ravenwood and squinted suspiciously through his glasses. "What are you doing here, Mister Ravenwood?"

"You know who I am?"

The elderly Whitfield nodded. "I'm familiar with your writings." He narrowed his eyes at Ravenwood. "I'll ask you again. What are you doing here?"

Before Ravenwood could answer, Darla stepped closer to her father. "I thought he may be able to help us."

"Your daughter told me about the Trumpet of Triton."

The professor looked alarmed and turned to his daughter. "You shouldn't have gone to him." He descended the last few steps on the staircase and stopped. "If you want to help, Ravenwood, take Darla to the station and see that she gets safely on board." He took her by the arm, and ushered her toward the door. Something caught his attention. "What's wrong with your eyes?"

"There was a terrible sound before tonight's quake," she said. "Just as Freddy described it."

"What are you talking about?"

"There was a series of loud harmonic tones followed by a strong tremor this evening," Ravenwood replied. "It struck downtown."

"Another one?" The professor had a far off look in his eyes. "How bad?"

"We left as it was happening, but it was causing quite a bit of damage," said Ravenwood. He reflected on the episode. "There was something strange about it. It seemed to be an isolated event."

The elderly Whitfield turned to his daughter. "You could have been killed!" He wavered.

Ravenwood rushed over and steadied him, spotted a chair, and ushered him over to it.

The professor collapsed in the seat, looking ill.

"Your daughter is still in danger," said Ravenwood.

The professor's concern-filled eyes stared up at him.

"She recognized a man on the elevator at my apartment building as one who has threatened you."

Whitfield's eyes darted. He stared at his daughter. "He followed you!"

"Sir, maybe you should tell me what's going on," said Ravenwood. "Is the man on the elevator responsible for the phenomenon causing the destruction?"

"I can't tell you." Whitfield looked up at him with worried eyes. "They'll kill her."

Ravenwood made his way over to the information desk and picked up the phone.

"What do you think you're doing?" Whitfield looked dumbstruck.

"I'm putting in a call to the local precinct." Ravenwood pressed the receiver to his ear to place the call, but the line was dead. Before he could return it to the cradle the professor pulled his gun. A second later, he had the open bore pointed at Ravenwood's head.

Darla looked stunned. "Father, what are you doing?"

"Put it down." The elderly man's gun wielding hand trembled. "Now."

She looked panicked. "Please, Ravenwood, do as he says."

Slowly, he placed the earpiece back in its cradle.

"Now, take my daughter to the train station and see that she gets safely onboard."

"I'm not leaving," she said.

"I won't take her against her will."

"Do it!" He cocked the hammer back.

"STOP!" She held out her hand. "I'll go!" She lowered her hand. "Just put the gun away."

The professor lowered it, but kept his finger curled around the trigger and watched as Ravenwood retrieved her bag from the floor.

She took a step toward her father.

"Go!" He waved her off.

Looking confused, she stopped. Miss Whitfield opened her mouth to speak.

"I said go."

She looked hurt.

"We should leave." Ravenwood took her by the arm and escorted her back to his car.

They drove awhile before she found her tongue again. She wrinkled her brow. "I've never seen him like this before." She turned to Ravenwood. "Why is he treating me like this?"

"He's afraid for you."

She seemed to take it in and grew quiet.

As they drove toward the train station, she watched the darkened city through the windshield. Cars were still out in numbers on the roads. The traffic slowed. Ahead, a crew of traffic cops were strung along the street working diligently to keep the flow steady and safe.

One motioned for the approaching Ravenwood to stop. When he did, the officer rapped the end of his nightstick against the glass. Ravenwood rolled down the window.

The officer leaned into the open hole. He glanced at Miss Whitfield before his gaze settled on Ravenwood. "Where are you heading?"

Darla leaned toward the window until she had a clear view of the officer. "We're on out way to the train station."

"The trains aren't running until power is restored."

"How soon will that be?" asked Ravenwood.

The officer shrugged. "That'll be up to the linemen, but I've got a pretty good hunch that the trains probably won't run tonight."

"We can go there and wait for the station to open," said Ravenwood.

The cop shook his head. "It will take you hours to make it through this traffic. The best thing you folks can do is go home until things get back to normal."

"That settles it." Darla sat up straight. "Take me back to the museum."

The officer looked satisfied. "Smart girl." He walked away.

Ravenwood waited for a break in the flow of traffic and turned the car around. They crept along. Exhaust fumes filled the air. "I know another way," said Ravenwood. "A back way." He took the first available right. It was an alley, narrow and dark.

"Are you sure we can make it through here?" she asked.

The roadster clipped a garbage can and knocked it over. The clatter of metal sang out loud. "I hope so." The corridor was long and populated with riffraff. Eyes were on them as Ravenwood edged past.

"Can't you go any faster?" she asked.

The beams from his roadster's headlights unveiled misaligned clutter in the alley. "Not without running into something, or someone."

At last they emerged and Ravenwood hooked a left. The street was dark and deserted, littered with trash and scraps of paper that the breeze set in motion like tumbleweeds. The place looked like a ghost town. The new route took them back into the city and back toward the museum. Along the way, Ravenwood happened to glance in the rearview. It framed a pair of headlights piercing the darkness. "There's a car speeding up behind us."

She quickly wheeled her head around and stared. "Do you think someone is following us?"

"I don't know, but there's one way to find out." He eased up off the gas. The vehicle in question matched the speed of the roadster.

He had a gut feeling that it was the man from the elevator. Their pursuer began to close the gap between them. Ravenwood could hear the roar of the car's engine as it sidled up to the driver's side. His hunch was right. The driver's electric blue eyes narrowed and his lips curled back in a primal snarl as he inched his vehicle closer.

"He's going to run us off the road!" she screamed. To their right, dark buildings towered over them. At this speed they'd be crushed upon impact.

Ravenwood pushed the pedal to the floor and edged ahead, but the car caught up. "Look for a turn."

She strained to see. "There!" Yards ahead was an intersection.

Tires wailed and the roadster shuddered as he yanked the wheel and veered to the right at a breakneck speed. The pursuing car, unable to make the turn, jetted past them. Ravenwood got the roadster under control and slowed it down to a manageable speed.

She breathed a sigh of relief.

He checked the rearview. "He's back on our tail."

She glanced back over her shoulder. "What do we do, now?"

"Hold on, I'm going to try and shake him." He mashed down on the accelerator again. The high performance engine hurled Ravenwood's coupe through the night at an unbridled speed. Once again, he checked the rearview. Behind, the vehicle matched his mad velocity. Together, they roared like wheeled cyclones through the streets with tires wailing on the curves, motors whining at their peak performance, as they raced forward. His coupe's headlights lanced the darkness barely revealing sudden changes in the layout of the streets. Ahead, a sharp turn. He cut the wheel.

Terror filled Miss Whitfield's eyes. "STOP!" The road ahead came to an abrupt end.

Immediately, Ravenwood slammed on the brakes. Rubber bit into the road, tires squalled as the roadster slid forward and chafed the pavement. The chase ended when the black sedan rocketed past them and smashed through the wire barricade surrounding a construction site. The car bucked across the uneven terrain and crashed into a bulldozer nose first. Briefly, the sound of crunching metal filled the air and collapsed back into silence. The radiator hissed as steam boiled from beneath the hood. A second later, the driver's door popped open and the big man emerged. The beams from the roadster's headlamps revealed him holding a gun.

Ravenwood quickly shifted into reverse, letting off the clutch as he gave the car gas. The spinning tires kicked up dust and gravel and the car lurched backward as a shot rang out.

He wheeled the car around and raced back toward the museum.

Breathing hard, Miss Whitfield clung to Ravenwood and buried her face in his shoulder.

It was highly unlikely for their pursuer to give chase anytime soon, but he kept a vigilant lookout in the rearview anyway. The mirror remained dark. Ravenwood parked and got out.

She quickly exited the passenger seat and hurried up the sidewalk while nervously looking back over her shoulder like she was expecting the black sedan to come screaming out of the darkness.

Ravenwood caught up to her at the door. It was locked. Keys rattled as she singled out the right one and jammed it in the keyhole. They walked in and caught Professor Whitfield standing in the glow of a lantern and in the act of scribbling on one of the walls with chalk.

He whirled around. With a look of surprise on his face, he asked, "What are you doing back?"

"The trains aren't running." Darla stared at the cryptic symbol repeatedly scrawled on the walls, hazy at best in the gloom. "What are these?"

The professor fidgeted with the chalk in his hand before he stuffed it inside his hip pocket. "Protection."

"It's an Apotropaic symbol." Ravenwood set the valise down and began examining one of the markings.

Darla shook her head. "I'm not familiar with the term."

"Supposedly it has the power to ward off evil."
He turned to Professor Whitfield. "Exactly who or what
are you dealing with?"

Whitfield scowled. "Enough of your meddling."
The professor pointed to the door. "Leave,
Ravenwood."

He stood rooted to the floor. "I'm afraid the
situation has become even more dire."

"What are you talking about?"

"The man who followed your daughter to
Sussex Towers just tried to run us off the road."

"And he took a shot at us." Miss Whitfield
remained visibly shaken.

The professor paled. "Where is he now?"

"He crashed his car at a construction site a few
miles back. But that won't stop him for long. You
should take your daughter and go someplace away
from the museum."

"She's safer here." He motioned to the symbols.

"I doubt very seriously your mystical renderings
will protect either of you, sir." Ravenwood shook his
head. "And you can't call anyone for help. The phones
are out."

"I have my gun." The professor gave his hip
pocket a pat. "And both Jake and the night watchman
are here."

"Sir, do you know what you're dealing with?"

"I know exactly what I'm dealing with. It's you
that doesn't understand."

Ravenwood stood in silence waiting for the
professor to expound.

Finally, the elderly Whitfield said, "The stakes are higher than you can imagine."

Ravenwood waited for more, but his silence only seemed to irritate the professor.

"Your prying is only complicating matters and slowing me down. I need time to think, and time is getting short." The professor looked on the edge of distress.

Darla stepped in. "You should go."

Ravenwood held his ground.

"I'll be fine." She assured him with what looked like a forced smile.

Ravenwood nodded and reluctantly let himself out. Clouds had stacked up. The skies had opened up and it was pouring rain. On the drive home, he hoped that the tremors had only produced minor damage and that no one was hurt. Concern for Porter, the elevator operator, Sterling, and his spiritual teacher, the Nameless One weighed heavily on his mind. Preoccupied by these thoughts, he lost track of time and space until the beams of his roadster revealed the broken, wire barricade. He slowed and peered through the deluge. Along with the man, the black sedan had vanished. Ravenwood sped away.

The roads, bound by traffic, slowly condensed, and then knotted as he approached the inner city. The street leading to Sussex Towers was littered with debris and clogged with police cruisers, an ambulance, and a cluster of officers. Gawking bystanders surrounded a group of nervous looking workers, dressed in slickers and hard hats, that stood outside the barricaded area of the open manhole. At the nucleus, Inspector Horatio Stagg pointed and shouting orders. Ravenwood was forced to park away from the commotion. His usual parking spot had been hijacked by a squad car. The only saving grace was a break in the downpour as he got out. As Ravenwood pushed through the police line, one of the officers took notice and rushed over.

The officer planted a hand on Ravenwood's chest. "You can't go in there, buddy."

"But, I live here. In the penthouse."

The cop gave Ravenwood's tailored suit the once over and looked as though he briefly toiled to make a decision. Finally, he replied. "I guess it'll be okay." He let his hand slide away.

During their brief discourse Stagg had broken away and was now approaching. The portly fellow eyed Ravenwood from beneath a set of thick eyebrows. There was grit in his expression. Ravenwood had seen the look plenty of times. "Excuse me, officer," said Ravenwood. He quickly slipped away.

"Hey, Ravenwood." It was Stagg's gruff voice. "Come back here. I want to talk to you."

He stopped.

The inspector walked at a brisk pace, the hard soles of his shoes striking the concrete with a fretful clatter. Once he caught up to Ravenwood, he stopped and peered up. "Someone cold-cocked the elevator operator."

"Is Porter all right?"

Stagg nodded. "He's got a lump on the side of

his head the size of the Empire State Building, but he's going to live." His dark eyes bored into Ravenwood's chameleon ones. "I've got a sneaking suspicion you know something about it."

"Inspector!" The voice came from behind.

Stagg turned. It was one of the officers.

"You're needed over here."

"I'll be there in a second," he yelled back. Stagg turned back to Ravenwood. "This place is a madhouse." He planted the tip of one of his thick fingers square on Ravenwood's chest. "You stay put until I get back." He turned and hurried away. Whatever Stagg wanted to tell him would have to wait.

Ravenwood headed for the entrance of his building and had to walk around the gumshoes barricading the manhole. Something caught his eye. He stopped and stared down. What little source of light made available by headlights was fractured by the surrounding crowd and set into constant motion by their movement. Ravenwood needed a flashlight and spotted an officer with one in hand. He walked over and without explanation plucked the light from the man's fingers. Before the officer could protest, Ravenwood ducked beneath the barricade and pushed his way through the crowd. A web of cracks spidered out from the manhole.

"Ravenwood!" Stagg's voice penetrated the ruckus, then he broke through the membrane of the crowd. With eyes fixed on his objective, he marched forward. Upon his arrival, Stagg said, "I need for you to talk to the crew that was working down in the storm sewer." He hiked his thumb and aimed it over his shoulder at the nervous looking bunch of workers now surrounded by news hounds.

"I have something more urgent," Ravenwood pointed out the cracks.

Stagg's eyes suddenly rounded out big. He raced to one of the cruisers, quickly scaled to the roof, and stood straddled over the red flashing light. He raised his hands high in the air and hailed the crowd, "Listen to me!" The din of voices continued. He freed his handgun from its holster and fired a shot into the air. Immediately, the chaos ceased. "Clear away from this area. There is a possibility of a cave-in." The commotion of voices swelled again, but this time electrified with fear. The crowd rippled out. He jumped to the ground and held his hands out. "Stop! Stay calm!" Stagg was caught in the living tsunami and swept away.

With the street now clear, Ravenwood returned to the manhole, got down on his knees, and poked the light down in the opening. The stone-lined throat of the well was cracked, but not bad enough for the place to cave in. He panned the light. It crawled across the subterranean walkway and revealed fast-moving water. The beam intercepted something slipping through the torrent. It was only a glimpse before his light flickered and winked out. He tapped the head against his open palm and it winked back on, but whatever he'd seen, or thought he'd seen, was now gone. Ravenwood prepared to climb down and investigate. A tap on the back of his shoulder stopped him. He looked up at the man.

"What do you think you're doing?"

A traffic cop stood over him, glaring down, while repeatedly tapping his nightstick against his open palm. It was the same cop that had stopped him and Miss Whitfield earlier that evening. The officer had migrated downtown. Behind him was a small band of firefighters.

"Well?"

Ravenwood pointed out the cracks.

"You ain't telling us something we don't already know." The flatfoot stopped drumming the nightstick. "I suggest you move along, and if I see you out here again, I'll run you in."

Ravenwood left. He walked through Sussex Towers' unguarded doors. Inside, battery powered lanterns scattered around the lobby illuminated the room. He approached a few blue-uniformed officers engaged in conversation. One broke away from the discussion, stepped out, and blocked Ravenwood's path.

Ravenwood said, "I'm a resident here."

The officer waved to the concierge behind the desk and after he had his attention the officer pointed to Ravenwood. After the concierge gave the okay signal the officer let Ravenwood pass.

With borrowed flashlight in hand, he made the long haul up the stairs to his penthouse. Inside, Sterling was waiting with a worried look on his face. He held a candle in a brass holder. "Thank goodness!" The breath of his exclamation jiggled the flame. He placed the candle on the foyer table and took his master's rain-soaked coat. "There was an earthquake, and then, when I didn't hear from you—"

"I'm fine, Sterling." The butler looked unscathed by tonight's events, but he asked anyway. "How are you?"

"I'm fine, sir." The butler's face still held concern. "But most of the lights were broken."

"Not to worry, Sterling, maintenance will replace them."

"Then I suppose you will be having dinner, sir?"

The evening's events had leached Ravenwood's appetite. He shook his head. "I'm not very hungry." With all concern for his manservant quelled, Ravenwood placed his hat and gloves next to the walking stick and marched off, leaving the disgruntled butler in a puddle of water. Although he felt the shaman wasn't harmed. Ravenwood still felt the urge to check on the Nameless One. He felt a magnetic tug as he strolled to the end of the hall.

As he walked the length of the hall, a scene still clear after fifteen years came to him. The mountainous crags of Burma, near the border of forbidden Tibet, and his father's hunting camp. A sound on the trail had startled them. Because prowling tigers were near, his father had lifted his gun, and curled a finger around the trigger. Instead of a beast, a man had appeared.

Bewildered, they watched as the hoary-headed being walked toward them. Bewildered because there was no settlement within miles, yet the lone man walked empty handed. It would have been near impossible for a man to survive such a trek alone and unarmed. A tiger had appeared behind the traveler, still distant, but striking toward the snowy-bearded man with lightning swiftness. Ravenwood's father, unable to get a clear shot had to wait. Finally, he fired, and a second later the extended claws of the tiger had dropped within an inch of the pilgrim. Paws which would have torn the old native to shreds fell limp. The ancient one had lifted his luminous eyes, and in his native tongue he had said: Always the Nameless One will guard you and your flesh. He then vanished from the trail as mysteriously as he had appeared.

After Ravenwood's parents perished during the Burmese Plague, the mysterious sage appeared again to fulfill his promise and cared for the orphaned boy.

Ravenwood emerged from the memory and stood outside the closed door.

Come, said the voice inside his head.

As the door parted the frame, an apron of light crawled across the floor and stalled a few feet inside the room. Ravenwood entered and mingled with the gloom as he trekked over to the Nameless One, postured on the floor—sitting crossed legged, head bowed. The shaman's white beard shrouded his chest until the hoary-headed mystic raised his chin and revealed a pair of luminescent eyes that fixed upon his visitor with a vaporous stare.

Sit came the word.

The voice was outside and omnipresent, yet contained inside Ravenwood's mind. He took the space in front of the shaman and emulated his posture.

Once again, the Nameless One stepped across the boundaries of his consciousness. *What was once buried beneath the waves of a great ocean yearns to rise again.*

"Help me to understand your words, master."

Soon, it will take shape and shake you with fear.

"What is this that you speak of?"

You mustn't allow fear and doubt to cloud your mind, my son. The world is at the threshold of change. The link is a man. He is both the serpent and the dagger.

"Siva clouds my mind, my teacher."

You exist in two places, my son. You exist with one foot in the spirit world and one foot in the world of form. Your Western traditions have taught you to rely solely on the five senses. As a student, you must learn to balance between the two worlds.

"What must I do to accomplish this?"

The Nameless One spoke nothing else, but bowed his head and closed his luminescent eyes.

Ravenwood stood, quietly let himself out, and returned to his library where he stationed himself at one of the windows and stared down. Hardworking linemen labored to restore electricity. He watched one daredevil walk an overhead wire like a tightrope. As attention-grabbing as this feat was, his eyes were again drawn to the manhole cover. The predominant cracks around it left him wondering why he had an overwhelming feeling he should be looking there for answers. Finally, he pulled himself away from the sight and left the room. Ravenwood knew that Sterling loved to read and was a walking encyclopedia of the city, his adoptive home. Guided by his flashlight, he stood in front of Sterling's bedroom door, made a fist, and prepared to knock, but changed his mind. Instead, he opened the door and shined the light over the sleeping butler.

Sterling restlessly stirred and pulled the cover over his head.

Ravenwood walked over and sat on the edge of the bed and tapped the lump where he thought a shoulder was.

The sleeping man popped up and stared at Ravenwood with a baffled look on his face. "Sir? Is something the matter?"

"What do you know about the storm sewers?"

"The storm sewers?" He continued to look perplexed. "Anything in particular, sir?"

"Are you familiar with the layout?"

"Why yes. The main channel runs through the heart of the city. Run-off water from all the other storm drains flows into it. From there it dumps into the ocean."

"Thanks." Ravenwood rose. "Go back to sleep, Sterling." He gave the butler another pat on the shoulder.

The puzzled butler watched him leave.

Ravenwood returned to his library and paced the floor, occasionally glancing out the window. The crews persisted with their work, and with the traffic cop hovering around the area, there was no going back down. Around two in the morning, he gave up the ghost and climbed into bed. At first, he lay there. Thoughts zipped through his head until he was able to clear them. Now in a condition of what the Nameless called a state of no mind, Ravenwood was able to penetrate the veil and found himself standing down in the sewer. The presence of the Nameless One came as a glowing orb of light that lit the subterranean cavern. Suddenly, the water began to glow. Something large was beneath the surface and in a few seconds it would reveal itself. A figure stepped out of the darkness and stood at the edge of the penumbra of light. A loud hum filled the air and shook the aqueduct.

"Sir?" A man's voice sounded as though it floated on a breeze from some faraway place. "Sir, wake up."

Ravenwood struggled through the veil of sleep and managed to crack open one eyelid. Sterling was shaking him on the shoulder and staring down at him with a look of concern on his face.

"Sir, you've overslept."

The visions in his head had faded back into the void. Ravenwood sat up. "I'm awake." As he rubbed the sleep from his eyes he noticed that lamp on his bedside table glowed. "Electricity has been restored."

"Yes, sir, and the phones are back in service as well."

"Then I guess things are getting back to normal." Ravenwood swung his legs out of bed and planted his bare feet on the floor.

"Yes, sir, and you have a meeting at nine sharp with the board members of the Metropolitan Bank."

"Yes—yes. I remember." He applied a long stretch and a yawn to his reply. "But someone is about to call and change those plans." The candlestick phone on his nightstand rang.

Even though Ravenwood had performed this feat on many other occasions, Sterling still looked stunned by the accuracy of his prediction.

Ravenwood grabbed the instrument and pressed the handset to his ear. It was Stagg. After the initial greeting, Ravenwood spent the next minute listening to the voice at the other end. When he hung up, he popped up off the bed. "Call the bank and relay the message that I can't make it."

"What reason should I give them?"

"It doesn't matter, Sterling. Make up something, if you have to."

"But, sir, that would be an untruth. I—I don't think I could do that. A gentleman should always be impeccable with his word. If I may be so bold to say."

"Well, explain that an emergency came up."

"Yes, sir." The puzzled look came back. "What type of an emergency?"

"Tell them that I have to go see an ailing friend. And that's the truth." Inspector Horatio Stagg always got a sick look on his face when he saw Ravenwood come through his office door, even when he was expected.

"Yes, sir." Sterling did a well-executed about-face and exited the room.

———

Thirty minutes later, Ravenwood was dressed in one of his tailored suits and speeding toward the precinct with the slipstream of air whipping the locks of his wavy, brown hair. He pulled to a stop at the curb and hopped out.

When he pushed through the glass door, the precinct was buzzing like a hornet's nest. A typical workday. Mischief was always brewing in Manhattan. One of the female clerks carrying a stack of papers collided with him and bounced off his tempered physique. At first, she appeared annoyed, but once her green eyes traveled up his body from the tip of his leather spats and settled on his chameleon eyes, she gave him a smile of approval and went about her business.

Ravenwood didn't need to ask for directions, he knew the way to Stagg's office. It was the last door on the left at the end of the long hall, and when he barged in, the inspector looked up from the paperwork on his desk and grimaced.

"What can I do for you, Dapper Dan?"

"You called me."

"Oh yeah, so I did."

"So, why am I here?"

The inspector grabbed the newspaper. "Look at this." He turned it around.

Ravenwood read the headline aloud: "Tremors shake Manhattan," and replied to it with, "Yes, I know. I was there, with you. Remember?"

"Not that article." The paper rattled repeatedly as Stagg's rapid-fire finger tapped on the smaller print at the bottom of the page. "This one."

Ravenwood took the paper, but this time he read to himself: Amphibious Creature Terrorizes Workers Down in Manhattan Sewer System. He quickly became absorbed in the article. While perusing it, Stagg interjected a hypothesis.

"It's probably someone's pet, baby alligator that got flushed down the toilet. I hear they can grow up to fifteen feet or more in the sewer."

Ravenwood stopped reading and looked up. "The workers described something much bigger than an alligator. They think it's some kind of sea monster." He thought about his glimpse of something slipping through the dark waters. Ravenwood raised an eye brow. "Do you believe in the paranormal now, Inspector?"

"No." Stagg frowned. "I think it's a hoax. But you know how people in this city go loony tunes when something odd happens. One freaky rumor leads to the next one. Then one of those news hawks gets a hold of it," he slapped the paper, "and spreads it across the front page of The Chronicle. And next thing you know," he waved his hands in the air, "there's panic in the streets." He let his hands fall to his sides.

Ravenwood returned to the article. "It says here, that before the sighting, a loud hum was heard by the crew." He read the time of the incident. "That's the same time the tremors occurred. The crew must have been petrified."

"From what I heard they came flying out of there. Look," said Stagg. "We need to stop this thing from taking off like a wild fire. Everyone is already in a stir. They think it's Armageddon! What do you think?"

Ravenwood had his head buried in the paper.

Stagg snatched it from his hand. "Are you listening to me?"

"I heard every word you said, Inspector."

"All this hocus pocus jazz is your field of expertise."

Ravenwood quickly interpreted the inspector's undertone. "Are you asking for my help?"

Stagg's head bobbled around before it settled on a nod. "Yeah."

Ravenwood considered the proposition. The prospect of investigating the paranormal dangled like an irresistible lure. He might even get fresh material for a new book, and the possibility the incident down in the storm sewer was linked to Darla Whitfield's problem hooked him. He could help her indirectly. Ravenwood nodded.

"Good." For the first time since Ravenwood entered the man's office, Stagg smiled. The inspector leaned forward and placed a finger on the button of the squawk box. "Susie, send Detective Kolchak to my office pronto."

"What are you doing?"

"I'm assigning one of my detectives to work with you on this."

"I work alone," said Ravenwood.

"You're on my dime now, so my rules," Stagg replied back. "I've got to give the appearance that I'm taking this matter seriously. Kolchak will provide that illusion."

A rap on the door preceded a man wearing a rumpled seersucker suit accented with a cheap necktie. His short-cropped, brown locks were topped with a ridiculous looking straw hat. He looked Ravenwood over through bloodshot eyes as he entered the room.

Stagg's gaze jumped between Kolchak and Ravenwood. "What's with the bloodshot eyes?"

Ravenwood didn't supply an explanation. The detective pawned it off as lack of sleep and then went on to rub the stubble on his chin. His gaze shifted to Stagg. "You wanted to see me?"

"Yeah." Stagg introduced them and explained the situation to the detective.

With a look of disdain, Kolchack said, "Come on, Inspector, there's real crime in this city. Why waste the taxpayer's money on some bogus monster hunt?"

"I'm not arguing with you on this, Detective." Stagg reached inside his desk drawer and pulled out a note pad. He tossed it to Kolchak. "Here is a list of the witnesses that claimed to have seen that thing." The inspector aimed his finger at the door. "Get going."

As they walked out, Kolchack asked, "So, what do we do now? Light candles? Sit on the floor crossed legged? Chant?"

Ravenwood endured the detective's taunting with reserve. "Let's just work together, solve this, so you can get back to your civic duties."

"The sooner the better," Kolchack shot back, "but let's get one thing straight. You follow my lead."

Ravenwood looked at his new partner as an added appendage, an unwanted one. Ravenwood felt his own experience with the paranormal would be paramount in solving this case, and since he already had an idea of where to start looking for answers, he had to find a way to lead from behind. Until then, to ease some of the friction, Ravenwood readily agreed.

"I'll do the driving." Kolchak pushed through the exit door.

They were met by a wave of mid-June heat. Ravenwood followed the detective down the concrete steps to a beat-up car parked next to the curb. It was a nineteen-twenty three Peerless motor car, green at one time, but now, oxidized, it looked like a moldy pickle.

"She might look like a flivver, but she runs good." Kolchak rounded the front bumper making his way to the driver's side.

When Ravenwood opened the passenger door, an accumulated mass of clothes, old papers, and a coffee mug tumbled to the ground. The cup shattered upon impact.

"I've been meaning to take those things out." Kolchak walked back to where Ravenwood stood and scooped the pile off the ground. "I'll put these in the trunk." A moment later, he returned to the driver's side empty-handed and climbed behind the wheel. On the third try, the car started. He stared at Ravenwood through the open door, sending out vibes of impatience. "Well, what are you waiting for?"

The car died.

Kolchak made several attempts to start the engine while rapping his fist against the dashboard. It still didn't start.

"That's okay," Ravenwood offered, "let's take my car."

Begrudgingly, the detective followed Ravenwood to his vehicle. Kolchak looked it over. "Nice car."

"Thanks. I had it custom-built."

The detective smirked. "Imagine that."

Ravenwood let the dig roll off his back and got in the car. After Kolchak climbed into the passenger seat and settled in, Ravenwood pressed the starter thinking that he would have to play along for a while. Then he could freelance on his own. "Where to?"

The detective reached inside the breast pocket of his jacket, pulled out the list of witnesses. He read off the first name and address.

The engine sang as Ravenwood drove away. He did a quick scan for traffic, and without warning, whipped the car around. Now on course, he headed for the inner city where the expensive roadster drew stares from the destitute.

"This is the place," said Kolchak.

Ravenwood whipped the car to the curb and got out. Long strides propelled him up the sidewalk to the doors of a dilapidated high rise. A few of the more notable building code infractions were broken windows and the fire escape that zigzagged up the outside wall like a rusty vine.

"Hey!" Kolchak called out.

Ravenwood stopped and turned around.

"Maybe one of us should stay here and look after your car."

"It will be fine," Ravenwood assured him. He spun back around and resumed his walk.

"No skin off my nose," Kolchak replied. "But I hope you've got cash for a taxi." He hurried and caught up just as Ravenwood entered the building.

Inside, the small lobby was dark and dank. A man, dressed in well-worn coveralls, was slapping some paint on the walls. A floor fan stood buzzing within a few feet of him. The torrent of air fluttered the wisps of long hair on the sides of his head making him look like some kind of odd flying creature. He suspiciously eyed Ravenwood and Kolchak as they walked by.

Ravenwood turned to the detective. "Which floor?"

Kolchak took a glance at the paper in his hand. "Third. Apartment three-C."

"Could I help you, fellas?" asked the painter.

They stopped and Kolchak nodded while looking around. "Yeah." His eyes came back to the worker. "Is there an elevator in this joint?"

"Yeah," the man replied back. "Over there." He pointed. "Around the corner. But, it don't work." He pointed to a recessed stairwell. "You'll have to take the stairs," he added as if it was he who would have to make the climb.

"Figures," Kolchak shot back.

The first step groaned when Ravenwood planted a foot on it. He felt the man's stare on the back of his neck until they were out of sight.

On the third floor, most doors were open to coax a breeze, but it did little to alleviate the stifling heat that conjured up odors and left them hanging in the hall. As they walked the narrow corridor, babies cried, a radio announced the Chicago Cubs upset over the Brooklyn Dodgers in a nine inning game, and an argument between a couple escalated into breaking glass. Ravenwood's sharpened senses honed in on the few miscreants loitering the hall. Their eyes followed as they passed.

"Three C." Kolchak sounded relieved as he rapped on the frame of the open door.

By late afternoon, Ravenwood and the detective had driven to each address and interviewed three of the witnesses. All claimed to have seen a leviathan down in the sewers. Even though each description of the thing varied slightly, a few characteristics were consistent: It appeared to be an amphibious creature with an enormous tail fin and had a single eye in the center of its forehead. And subsequent to the creature's appearance, they had all heard a strange hum.

"It sounded like one, long blast of a trumpet," said Sean Deloney, the fourth man and last man they interviewed. He was a stout, young lad with fiery red hair and a notable accent that leaned toward Irish heritage. He looked anguished reliving the tale as he sat uncomfortably in a wooden rocker next to a Dalston nesting table, host to a Bible and picture of an elderly woman. A string of rosary beads draped across the frame.

"I'm sorry to put you through this again," said Ravenwood. "Thank you for your time, Mister Deloney." He and Kolchak stood to leave.

"Wait," said Sean.

Ravenwood paused, waiting.

"Do you think—" The boy's eyes strayed from Ravenwood's chameleon ones as he turned his face down and his gaze settled on the scuffed toes of his stained work boots.

"It's all right, son," said Ravenwood. "You can confide in me and Detective Kolchak here."

"Me Mum used to read to us from this Bible." He picked up the well-worn, leather-clad book from the nesting table. "In Revelations it talks about the seven trumpets." Deep-rooted fear surfaced in his green eyes.

"And you think it's the end of days?" Kolchak asked. He grinned.

The young lad nodded. "You do believe in God and His holy words, don't you?"

"I believe there's a reasonable explanation for all of this," Ravenwood replied. "And Detective Kolchak and myself are going to find out the cause."

After they left the small, modest apartment, Kolchak asked, "Do you really believe that load of bull?"

"The part about the Bible or the leviathan?"

Kolchak looked flabbergasted by the question, but quickly recovered and leveled his narrowed-down eyes at Ravenwood. "I'll have you know that I'm a Christian man."

"So, you think it's the seven trumpets of Armageddon?"

The detective blinked staccato. "Well — No — I mean, yeah. I mean, I believe what the Bible teaches, but the end of the world is something in the far-off future." He straightened his spine and lifted his chin. "Look, Ravenwood, you know what I was asking you."

"I'm not sure what to believe just yet," he answered, "but I know there are possibilities beyond our realm of reasoning."

"Come on, a one-eyed sea monster?" He took a pause. "You know what I think?"

Ravenwood got into his car.

Kolchak rode shotgun. "More than likely they had been sipping on some homemade hooch down there and had a figment of the imagination. It's the evening shift and no supervisors. It makes sense, doesn't it?"

"As much as anything else does right now. Where to?" asked Ravenwood.

Kolchak huffed. "The precinct. I'm throwing in the towel on this one. Stagg can call me onto the carpet if he wants, but I've had enough of this magic act."

Ravenwood let out a sigh of relief. The detective must have heard.

"You and me both, pal," Kolchak said as he looked at his watch. "Hey, my shift will be over at five. How 'bout we go get a cup of coffee instead and I'll jot down some notes for my daily report?"

Ravenwood took in the officer's lightened mood. "Suits me just fine."

"But you're buying, rich boy." Kolchak flopped back in the seat. "I know a dining car not too far from here."

Ravenwood followed the detective's directions to Joe's; a sleek, silver-skin caboose with striped awnings. He peeled from the congested street traffic and parked next to the curb. Skyscrapers towered behind the eatery like a field of overgrown weeds. Across the street, the Manhattan Bay, trimmed with long docks and metal warehouses that glistened under a hot sun, was busy with boats of all sizes churning around.

Kolchak jumped out and stood in the middle of the sidewalk flowing with pedestrian traffic. "Isn't this great?"

Ravenwood remained behind the wheel and stared at the place.

"I know, this ain't a tea and crumpet on a doily kind of place, but the java's hot and the waitress is cute as a button." He walked inside.

A record spun on the jukebox, and the sound of jazz mingled with the jumbled voices of diner patrons as they talked about the earthquake. The waitress behind the counter snuffed her cigarette and walked over to the detective.

"Hi'ya, Mabel." Kolchak slung his hat on the rack.

"Hi, yourself. How's your boy doing?"

"Good. Growing like a weed. He's almost ten."

Ravenwood approached and stood next to the detective.

The perky blonde turned on her charm with a million dollar smile as she looked Ravenwood over. "So who's your friend, Leonard."

"This is Ravenwood."

"Nice to meet you, honey." She purred through a red lipstick smile.

Ravenwood nodded. "Likewise." By the look on her face, his curt response had been like a slap across her cheek. Evidently the flirtatious waitress was used to wrapping most men around her little finger.

She quickly recovered and her bubbly smile returned. "Oh—kay. What can I get for you gentlemen?"

"Coffee," answered Kolchak.

"Have a seat and I'll have it right out." She turned to walk away.

"Mabel," Kolchak called out.

She turned.

"Got any of that fancy brew for my friend here?"

"We've got coffee, and you're in luck, it was made this morning." She smirked, did a whirl, and walked off.

"Over there." Kolchak pointed to an empty booth next to a window.

As they waded through the smoky haze, Kolchak hummed along with the sultry voice of Billie Holiday singing the song *Summertime*. They settled in.

Kolchak pulled a pen and a small leather-bound notepad from his pocket and plopped them on the scarred tabletop. He opened it, raised an eyebrow, and smirked. "How do you spell boogey man?"

Ravenwood ignored the ribbing from his soon to be ex-partner. When he came into the diner he'd heard Mabel mention something about Kolchak having a son. He looked at the thin, well-worn gold band around Kolchak's ring finger. He decided to initiate small talk. "So, you have a wife and son, Detective?"

Kolchak gently rubbed the ring with his fingertip. "I lost my wife three years ago." He opened his mouth to say something else but faltered.

Instantly, Ravenwood regretted meddling. "I'm very sorry for your loss."

The detective regained his composure, nodded, and said, "Now, it's just me and my boy."

Mabel returned juggling a cup and saucer in each hand. They rattled when she set them on the table. "Anything else, gentlemen?" She placed a hand on Ravenwood's shoulder.

"Well, since my partner here is buying—," Kolchak grabbed a menu and skimmed the choices. He looked up at the waitress. "I'll have a burger—all the way, and fries." He took a moment to give it some more thought. "And, a slice of lemon meringue pie." He looked over at Ravenwood. "What'll you have?"

"I'm not hungry."

"Suit yourself." The detective shrugged and tossed the menu back down.

"You don't know what you're missing." Mabel let her hand slip from Ravenwood's shoulder and stepped across the aisle. "How about you, Freddy, more coffee?" she asked the man occupying one of the barstools.

He looked at his watch. "I have to be at work soon, and I've got to foot it."

"You have time." She grabbed one of the carafes from the bar. As she poured, Mabel asked, "Why don't you quit that job after what happened the other night?"

"Can't," he replied. "I've got a family to take care of."

She placed the carafe back on the counter. "Well, if it were me, the folks at the Davis Museum would be looking for another night watchman."

Taken by surprise, Ravenwood turned and looked at the man. Then, as Mabel sashayed away, he spoke to the stranger. "Excuse me."

The man's back remained to Ravenwood.

"Freddy."

The man stopped stirring, and looked back over his shoulder. Both eyes were bloodshot, and he had a shiner beneath his left eye.

"My name's Ravenwood."

"I know who you are. I was around when you brought Miss Whitfield back to the museum last night."

It was the man that Ravenwood had felt watching him from the dark recesses. "I'd like to ask you a few questions about what happened."

—

Freddy scanned the room. The conversation had already piqued curiosity in a few nearby onlookers. "Not here." He stood and slapped a handful of change down on the counter. "See ya, Mabel," he told the waitress from across the bar and walked out.

Kolchak's face was brimming with curiosity as well. "What's going on, Ravenwood?"

He ignored the question and followed the man out the door.

"Hey, Mabel," Kolchak called out to the waitress. "Cancel that order." He grabbed his hat and rushed out in time to catch a glimpse of Ravenwood and Freddy disappearing around the back corner of the dining car.

Kolchak edged up to the corner and stopped. Concealed from view, he listened in. Ravenwood was talking.

"Do you know what's happening at the museum?"

"I can tell you what I know. A few nights ago, I heard noises coming from the basement, so I had to go down and check it out. The light bulbs were bursting and I saw a pair of green eyes staring at me."

Ravenwood dismissed the green-eyed creature as Jake prowling the premises.

"Then," said Freddy, "there was an overpowering sound vibrating through me until I was disoriented." He shuddered at the recollection. "I went out cold. I don't know how long I was unconscious, but when I came to, it felt like someone had dumped a load of cement inside my head. I managed to make my way through the dark and crawl up the stairs. Most of the lights and display cases were broken, and those two goons were standing in the middle of the lobby. Somehow they got past the locked door and demanded that I call the professor. When I refused they got rough with me and tossed me around like a rag doll. I ran back to the office and got his revolver, but when I got back up to the front they were gone." Freddy took out a pack of Lucky Strike cigarettes and lit one. "Since then, I've borrowed some protection." He patted his hip pocket.

Ravenwood could make out the faint outline of a handgun.

"You can't be too careful these days." He extended the pack of smokes to Ravenwood.

He waved it off. "Who were the men?"

Freddy shrugged and took a drag off the cigarette. "I don't know, but I watched them drive away in a black sedan." Freddy pointed the red tip of the cigarette at Ravenwood. "You want to know my take on those two goons?"

"Sure."

"They're mafia."

Ravenwood cocked his head.

"Trust me," said Freddy. "They just had that look." The conversation was momentarily interrupted by a long blast from a tugboat's steam whistle. When it was done, he added "And, they're Greek."

"What makes you say that?"

"They had Greek accents," replied Freddy.

"Are you certain?"

Freddy nodded. "I used to work the docks." He took a drag off the cigarette. "I recognized the accent." His words came out encapsulated in smoke and were ferried away by the breeze.

"Do you know what they wanted?"

"When I was making my way up the stairs, I caught a piece of the conversation they were having. I heard something about a stone." Freddy stared reflectively as he took a long pull off his Lucky Strike. "It could have been stones." His eyes lit up as he nodded his head. "Yeah, I bet the professor has precious stones locked up in that safe."

"Why didn't you call the police?"

"Do you think I want to end up fish food at the bottom of the river?" He shook his head. "No sir, I'm staying out of this." He looked at his watch. "I've got to get going, Ravenwood." He walked away and joined the flow of pedestrians. Within a few seconds the night watchman was gone.

Ravenwood stepped back around the corner. Kolchak was waiting for him.

The detective glared. "What else have you been keeping from me, Ravenwood?"

"It was you that didn't want to get involved, remember? " He walked to his roadster and climbed behind the wheel.

Kolchak followed and stuck his head through the open window of the passenger door. "Yeah, well, that was before extortion came into play, especially when it involves the mafia."

Ravenwood started to tell the detective that he

didn't need his help, but he was suddenly seized by the intuition that Kolchak would somehow play a pivotal role as the mystery unfolded. His logic played tug of war with his hunch. The voice of the Nameless One entered Ravenwood's head. *Trust your intuition, my son.* Finally, Ravenwood nodded his head. "Get in."

Kolchak jumped in the passenger seat.

The coupe left a trail of black tire marks as Ravenwood sailed out into the traffic under protest of screeching tires and the blare of car-horns. Now on the straightaway, the roadster gathered speed as the needle on the gauge arced. It wasn't until they were at the museum that Ravenwood slowed and then brought the car to a stop. He jumped out and rushed inside. The broken glass from the ceiling lights had been swept away. What remained of the working lights spackled the floor with dim light. "Professor! Miss Whitfield!" he called out. Silence reigned. Even Jake, the collie, wasn't there to bark at the intrusion. Ravenwood stepped further into the room.

Finally, a voice called out, "Freddy?" Whitfield, disheveled, entered the ill-lit chamber carrying a lantern in one hand and a gun in the other. "Is that you?" His gun hand trembled.

Kolchak was tucked in a shadow. "Easy, sir, put that away before you hurt someone."

The professor squinted at the darkness. "Who are you?"

"Detective Leonard Kolchak with the Manhattan Police Department." He waded into a scrap of light.

Whitfield narrowed his eyes and lowered the gun. "I didn't call for the police."

"He's with me," said Ravenwood, stepping forward.

"What are you doing here?" Whitfield scowled. "I told you to stay out of this."

"There's got to be a reason you don't want the police involved." Kolchak narrowed an eye at him. "Maybe you got some skeletons in the closet you don't want anyone to know about."

"I don't have anything to hide."

"We heard you have connections to the Greek mafia," Kolchak shot back.

"What?" Whitfield suddenly looked flustered. "What are you talking about?"

"Why don't you spill it, Professor?" The detective stared straight-faced. "It'll go a lot smoother for you if you cooperate."

"I don't know anything about the mafia," said Whitfield.

Darla strolled into the light and stopped. "What's this about the Greek mafia?"

"He knows." Kolchak pointed to the professor. "Your boy, Freddy, spilled the beans about the two men that showed up here wanting the precious stones you've got locked inside the museum's safe."

"There are no precious stones in the safe."

She shook her head. "And they're not mafia." Darla turned to her father. "Tell them who the men are."

The professor pressed his lips into a thin line.

"All right," said Miss Whitfield. "I'll tell them." She turned to Ravenwood. "They are Atlanteans."

Kolchak screwed up his face. "Like from Georgia?"

"Not Atlanta, Detective. Atlantis. Those men are descendents of the few who survived the destruction of the city of Atlantis," her tone serious. "Have you ever heard of it?"

"Yeah, from comic books."

She turned to Ravenwood. "The damage from the earthquakes here and downtown were a small demonstrations of the Trumpet's capabilities."

Kolchak looked at her. "What trumpet?"

"The Trumpet of Triton," said Ravenwood. He imparted the history of the myth to the detective.

At first, Kolchak looked dumbfounded, then he laughed again. "This sounds like something from one of those crazy movies my boy likes to watch." He chuckled. "And you're talking like it was a real place."

"At this point, we must assume it is real," Her tone was sharp. "Lives could be at stake."

"Whose lives?" Kolchak asked.

The professor surrendered his silence. "They are going to destroy Manhattan."

"If they have the trumpet," said Ravenwood, "then why are they threatening to destroy the borough?"

"They want the stones Freddy referred to. Only it's not precious stones. It's stone tablets, the codex of the trumpet."

"Whoa!" Kolchak raised his hands in the air. "There's a lot of holes that need filling in." He dropped his hands to his sides. "How about starting at the beginning."

The professor nodded. "All right. At the last archeological conference I attended, a man by the name of Jones confided in me that he believed the lost city of Atlantis lay at the bottom of the eastern Mediterranean within the Cyprus Basin, and he was going to find it." The professor went on to say, "And that was the last I'd heard from him until he showed here at the museum late one night with the tablets. He told me that the diving expedition had been a success and he had located the city's ruins. He said he had found both the Trumpet and the tablets enclosed in a stone vault and sealed with the mark of Triton."

The detective shrugged. "Is there something special about the mark?"

"It is a mystic blocking symbol used to prevent the Atlanteans from ever opening it."

Ravenwood speculated about this then added, "But there was nothing to stop a man that was not of Atlantean descent from opening the vault."

The professor nodded. "That is correct. Shortly after he'd retrieved the artifacts, the Trumpet was stolen from his home. Thankfully, Jones had the tablets in his office at the University as he was working on deciphering the inscriptions. Soon after the theft, two men contacted him offering a million dollars for the tablets. He refused their offer." He paused. The gap was quickly growing into a chasm of suspense as all eyes were on the professor. Finally, he spoke. "Jones felt nervous, so he went into hiding while he finished deciphering the codex. When he was done, he knew the full power of the Trumpet, and he knew that it would become an even more dangerous instrument in the wrong hands if they acquired the tablets as well."

Curiosity had grabbed hold of Kolchak. "What's on the tablets?"

"According to Jones, the Trumpet not only has the power to destroy cities, it possesses the power to restore them," the professor replied. "The codex explains how to reverse the polarity of the Trumpet. Once that knowledge is obtained, I believe the Atlanteans will attempt to raise their city from the ocean floor and resurrect their army from the dead."

Kolchak's eyes rounded out big. "You mean like zombies?"

"Necromancy," replied the professor.

The detective shook his head. "I don't know what that means."

"It means," said Ravenwood, "raising the deceased from the grave and making them whole again."

"But first they need the tablets in order to know how to proceed," the professor added.

"It all sounds crazy." Kolchak massaged his forehead.

"No one is asking you to believe a word of this," said Darla.

"Suppose it is true," said Kolchak. "Why didn't this fella, Jones, return the tablets back to the vault on the ocean floor where it would be safe?"

"He knew that if he did, they'd find someone else to retrieve the tablets," replied the professor. "And being ignorant of its content, they would gladly hand it over to the Atlanteans for the money."

"Assuming what he found is the genuine article, why bring it here?" Ravenwood asked.

"Two reasons," Whitfield replied. "He needed to give it to someone who would understand the gravity of the situation, and he wanted an obscure location."

"But someone must have been following him, like he said, on the night he brought the tablets," Darla added. "Two men showed up claiming to be collectors and offered the one million dollars to my father."

"Of course I knew better," said the professor. "And when I exposed their ruse, they threatened to destroy the entire city of Manhattan."

"The damage at the museum was the first warning," said Miss Whitfield.

"And the quake at Sussex Towers was the second," said Ravenwood, thoughtfully.

"What's to stop them from breaking into that safe of yours?" asked Kolchak.

"Even if they did, the museum is fortunate enough to possess an amphora protected by the mark of Triton."

"A what?" Kolchak stared at the professor from beneath a wrinkled brow.

63

"It's a jar," replied the professor. "It came from one of the ancient temples of Greece, and it's large enough to place the codex inside."

"So, the only way for them to get their hands on the tablets is for you to hand them over," said Kolchak.

The professor nodded. "I have less than six hours."

"What are we going to do?" Miss Whitfield's blue eyes were filled with concern.

"We'll have to find them first," said Ravenwood.

"How?" she asked. "We don't know where to look."

"I do," replied Ravenwood. "They're in the aqueducts below the city." Suddenly, he paused. He sensed a presence. Hidden eyes had been watching them. A man made invisible by the dark. The figure emerged from the gloom, a familiar face.

Whitfield smiled. "Freddy. I didn't hear you come in." He pulled out his pocket watch. "You're early."

Freddy shook his head. "Actually, I'm right on time."

As Freddy walked past, Ravenwood noticed the night watchman had rolled up the sleeves of his shirt, exposing the markings on his forearm: a snake coiled around a dagger.

The Nameless One issued a warning inside Ravenwood's mind: *Careful my son, the serpent is ready to strike.* Quickly, Ravenwood drew his Luger.

But the night watchman was already behind Miss Whitfield and swiftly cinched his arm tightly around her waist. He whipped the gun out of his pocket and pressed it to her head. Terror filled her blue eyes.

Kolchak pulled his gun as well and put the bead on the night watchman.

"Drop the guns!" Freddy cocked the trigger back. "Or she gets it."

"Please!" Professor Whitfield looked petrified. "Do as he says."

All three weapons hit the floor with a clatter.

"Kick those heaters over here."

The guns skittered across the floor and stopped at the tips of Freddy's shoes.

"Freddy, why are you doing this?" The professor looked bewildered.

"Because I'm tired of getting paid peanuts. I aim to collect that one million dollars and get my wife and kids out of that rat-infested trap on the east side."

"All right," said Whitfield. "Just don't harm my daughter."

Freddy turned the gun on Kolchak.

"If you kill us," said the detective, "that'll be a double homicide. They'll string you up for sure."

"Only if I get caught, and I'm going to make sure that ain't gonna happen."

"WAIT!"

Freddy turned the gun on the professor. "Shut up, old man."

"Please." The professor held out his hands. "Just listen."

"All right, but make it quick."

Whitfield lowered his hands. "Handcuff them."

"Be smart," said Ravenwood. "Do what he says and avoid a double murder rap."

"I don't have handcuffs."

"I have a set," said Kolchak. He slowly opened the lapel of his jacket and exposed them.

Freddy nodded. "All right. Slip one of the bracelets around your wrist."

Kolchak complied.

"Make sure it's tight."

The detective cinched it down another notch. "If I make it any tighter it'll cut off the circulation to my hand."

"Go stand over there." Freddy motioned to the vertical steam pipe running down to one of the floor radiators.

Again Kolchak did what he was told.

Freddy pointed the gun at Ravenwood. "Go stand on the other side."

When they were both in place, Freddy had Kolchak thread the open cuff between the wall and the pipe and then had Ravenwood lock it around his wrist. "Keys," said Freddy.

Kolchak tossed them and they landed at the night watchman's feet.

Satisfied, Freddy walked Darla over to them. "Would you have ever thought that a bohunk and a aristocrat teaming up together would make such a good team?"

She shook her head.

Freddy looked smug, pursed his lips together as he nodded his head. "But you know, you guys go together like peas and carrots." His smug look changed to an arrogant grin. "And that's why I can't take any chances of you getting free and following me." He cold-cocked them for good measure.

Ravenwood slipped into darkness. The next time he opened his eyes, he was sitting upright on the floor, slumped against the wall.

Kolchak groaned.

"Are you all right, Detective?"

Kolchak groaned again. "Yeah." He rubbed the lump on his head. "I think so." Then he struggled against his fetters. They rattled against the pipe. "How are we going to get out of the cuffs?"

Ravenwood popped up. His end of the handcuffs had been removed.

The detective looked up, astounded. "How'd you do that?"

Ravenwood shook his head. "I learned Houdini's trademark handcuff trick when I was a boy." He finished removing Kolchak's restraints and looked around the room. Miss Whitfield and the professor were nowhere in sight. He called out their names, but was answered by howls. "Jake!"

"It's coming from below." Kolchak rubbed his chafed wrist.

Together, they gathered their guns. Kolchack pocketed the keyless handcuffs and followed the ruckus to the basement.

Ravenwood was the first one down the stairs and to enter the room. "Professor! Miss Whitfield!" It was dark.

"Here." Kolchak reached around and stuffed a metal cylinder into Ravenwood's hand. "Use my flashlight."

With a push of the switch, he energized the bulb, and searched the room. The light washed across a person lying on the floor. Jake stood next to the man, whining.

Ravenwood rushed over and kneeled. "Sir?" He shook the man.

The elderly Whitfield groaned, stirred, sat up. and slapped the palm of his hand over his forehead. A little blood trickled from beneath his fingers. He moaned.

"Are you all right?"

The professor jumped to his feet and skimmed the room with frantic eyes. "He took Darla. You have to go after him."

"Where did he take her?" Kolchak looked around the room with a confused look on his face.

Jake barked. All three men raced to a row of wooden crates stacked head high, and when the rounded the corner the flashlight revealed the dog with his nose poked down an uncovered manhole. The sound of his yapping reverberated in the underground channel.

"Easy, boy," said Ravenwood. He restrained the dog by the collar and gently pushed the dog aside.

After Professor Whitfield took command of Jake, Ravenwood got down on his hands and knees and shined the light downward."

The detective suddenly looked terrified. "You're not thinking about going down there, are you?" He pointed out the network of jagged cracks that radiated out from the hole's circumference. "The place could cave in at any time!"

"I'm not asking you to go, Detective. You've done your part. You wait here with the professor."

"I'm going with you, Ravenwood!" Whitfield pushed past him and planted a foot on the first metal rung.

Ravenwood grabbed him by the arm and pulled him out. "You're staying here."

The professor wiggled free from Ravenwood's grip. "That's my daughter down there."

"I understand your worry, but I need for you to call Inspector Stagg, fill him in on what's going on, and lead him here when he arrives. Every second is crucial. Do you understand?"

Whitfield pointed at the detective. "He can do that."

Ravenwood looked to Kolchak. "Which is it going to be?"

"I swore an oath to protect the citizens of this city and that's what I'm going to do." Kolchak scrambled down the rungs.

"Don't worry," said Ravenwood. "You'll have to find your way back upstairs in the dark."

Whitfield nodded. "Jake will lead me."

"Hurry it up, would you?" Kolchak called up from the darkness.

Ravenwood went down the rungs. The electric glow of the flashlight filled the cavity as he waved it around.

The pale-looking detective stood at his side, slightly slumped, and staring up at the ceiling. Beads of sweat were popping out on his forehead. Cracks had compromised the integrity of the structure.

Ravenwood asked, "Can I count on you, Detective?"

Kolchak diverted his gaze back to Ravenwood. "Yeah." He straightened his shoulders. "Which way?" They were at an intersection.

Ravenwood turned the light downward and illuminated the walk. Fresh footprints were embossed in the green slime. "This way."

Kolchak followed.

Ravenwood aimed the light into the corridor and quickened his pace, careful not to stray too far to his right. One slip of the foot could send him over the edge and into the fast moving water. Suddenly, a warning from the Nameless One filled Ravenwood's mind—*Caution, my son. The jaws of death are near.* Across the water on the opposite bank, a dozen small, red, glowing dots tossed back the peripheral light. He turned the beam full on them. "Careful," he told the detective.

"Alligators!" Kolchak quickly pressed his back to the wall.

As Ravenwood's light skimmed over the white-skinned reptiles, one by one, the alligators slipped off the bank and into the water.

"Ravenwood!" Kolchak had found a new source for his panic. The detective danced away from the crisis. A few feet away he stopped, and with his heart still thumping hard inside his chest, Kolchak looked back. A small portion of the walkway was gone and the reptiles prowled the water. He slowly peeled his gaze from the alarming spectacle and turned to Ravenwood. "We're okay."

For now, thought Ravenwood. But the aqueduct was well over a hundred years old and subject to constant erosion. He hoped that they would get to Miss Whitfield before she fell victim to one of the insidious traps, or before she had served Freddy's purpose, and he disposed of her. The thought prompted him to hurry. He stepped across the gap and moved forward. Caution governed his speed.

Along the way, they came to a section where smaller aqueducts entered the main channel. Above their heads, runoff water spewed into the subterranean canal. The roar was deafening.

Ravenwood hugged the wall as he ducked behind the racing arcs of water and edged along, knowing that if the powerful geysers were to clip any part of his body, the force would shove him into the eddies where he'd be carried out to sea, or worse.

When they came out on the other side, Kolchak pointed. "Look." In the distance a staircase angled up from the walkway to a service door. It was closed, but light seeped from beneath the bottom gap and spilled down the steps. They approached cautiously, stopped at the base, staring up. Rust had eaten through several of the metal balusters.

Ravenwood tested the reliability of the structure with a shake. In return, it shrieked a hollow metallic note. The door jerked open.

Immediately, Ravenwood extinguished his light, and they ducked beneath the stairs. With their backs pressed to the wall, they watched an oscillating disc of light skim the walkway. The sound of footfalls coming down the steps echoed in the chamber. Ravenwood drew his gun. "Only if necessary," he muttered under his breath. There was a pause. Ravenwood looked up. Even though the risers eclipsed his view, he could see a pair of scuffed shoes. He'd have to wait for the man to come down and step out in the open before he could get a clear look at him. He might be nothing more than a city employee working on the system. The creeper did a one-eighty and went back up the stairs leaving the man's identity a mystery.

After the door closed, Kolchak whispered, "That was Freddy."

"How do you know?" Ravenwood whispered back.

"I recognized those beat-up pair of Hushpuppies. It was the same pair he was wearing this afternoon."

The two men waited before they scaled the edifice, careful not to make the cranky structure sing out and betray their approach. At the top, Ravenwood was met by the closed metal door. The yellow glow of incandescent light escaping through the gap at the bottom spilled out onto the first step. He got down on his belly.

Kolchak sidled up next to his partner and laid down on the hinged side of the door.

Ravenwood pressed an ear to the crack and heard voices. One was resolute and clear, the other, a tinny broadcast through a speaker — the brief gaps in between their conversation was filled by electronic hiss. Both had Greek accents. He parted the door a crack and pressed an eye to it.

Once, Ravenwood had seen a cathode ray tube. The instrument was capable of receiving a transmission and turning the signal into a moving picture. The one he was staring at now had captured the face of a man. The widow's peek of a silver helmet touched the top of his aquiline nose. His pale eyes were fixed on the man sitting in front of the screen clutching a microphone, at his elbow were the tablets. Freddy's and Miss Whitfield's presence remained hidden from view. Ravenwood hoped she was in there and not already disposed of. He pulled his Lugar, placed his hand on

73

the door, and whispered out, "Are you ready?"

"I don't think rushing in there like gangbusters is such a good idea," Kolchak whispered back.

"Under the circumstances, I don't think that we have any other choice." Ravenwood shoved and the door's cranky hinges heralded their intrusion.

The man sitting in front of a small television screen whirled around. He wore a frown encased by a silver beard.

Both Ravenwood and Kolchak jumped to their feet.

As the door continued to arc inward, the growing gap revealed Darla. She stood in the corner with her ankles and wrists cast in iron bracelets with an extra length of chain tethered to her wrist, and the hem of her dress had been torn away and used as a gag. She spotted Ravenwood. Her eyes suddenly filled with terror as she issued a muffled scream and feverishly shook her head. The growing gap bared Freddy holding a gun. He smiled.

A shot rang out, and a bullet split the air.

Freddy's nefarious grin disintegrated as a red spot appeared on his chest and spread across his shirt. He slumped, buckled at the knees, and crumbled to the floor.

The sound of the gun being fired had come from behind. It left a ringing in Ravenwood's ears. He looked back over his shoulder. Kolchak held a smoking gun. At that moment, Ravenwood's heightened senses picked up death. He whirled back around.

The robed giant had jumped to his feet and had pulled a futuristic blunderbuss pistol. He pulled the trigger.

Suddenly, the door jamb at Kolchak's side screeched and burst apart. Even though the giants mark had been slightly off, the ear-shattering harmonics slammed into their bodies like a tidal wave. The impact flung Ravenwood's gun from his stinging hand. He heard Kolchak let out a gasp and go tumbling down the stairs.

The man beaded on Ravenwood's midsection.

Ravenwood lunged and collided with the Atlantean. The impact sent them both to the floor and the weapon sailing across the room.

In seconds, Ravenwood was back on his feet.

So was the giant. He plunged headlong toward Ravenwood with murder in his eyes.

Ravenwood coiled his hands into tight fists. The man stood a foot taller and outweighed him as much as fifty pounds of solid muscle. Now, within arms length, the Goliath threw a punch.

Ravenwood blocked the bone-crushing blow with his left forearm and delivered a haymaker. *SMACK!* The giant's eyes glazed. But the triumph was short lived. The glassy look in his eyes disappeared. He grinned, exposing two rows of broad, blood-coated teeth. Ravenwood dodged the incoming blow, felt the brush of air against his cheek. Every man has his Achilles heel. Ravenwood just had to spot it. He had seconds. It came.

The man dipped his right shoulder as he drew back his fist. The move exposed the Atlantean's midsection. Ravenwood delivered a quick punch, this time to the man's solar plexus. The giant doubled over while clutching his belly. With lightning speed, Ravenwood rushed over, snatched the giant's weapon off the floor and now had the flared end of the gun aimed.

With a look of scorn in his eyes and teeth gritted the Atlantean rushed him.

Ravenwood pulled the trigger. In that second, along with the high-pitched screech emitted from the end of the barrel, he heard the thick, heavy choke of bursting flesh.

Miss Whitfield had worked free of the gag binding her voice and let out a loud, long scream.

Ravenwood dropped the gun and rushed to her side. "It's all right now, Miss Whitfield. I'm going to get you out of here."

Her eyes, filled with terror, remained fixed on the blob of gray/pink matter and splintered bone heaped on the floor.

As he took her by the arm she fell against him sobbing. Ravenwood gathered up the tablets and did the best he could to shield her from the sight as he escorted her out of the room now filled with the heady odor of death.

Her steps punctuated by the shackles and the extra length of chain dragging the stairs became a daunting task as he led her down. Kolchak was nowhere to be seen, but again his radar picked up on something other than the detective. Instantly, he knew who it was, but it was too late. He heard a click. Ravenwood recognized it. It was the sound of a gun hammer being cocked back. Slowly, he turned his head.

Freddy stood behind them. His descent down the stairs was marked by a trail of blood. He held his gun against Darla's head. "Give me the tablets."

He shoved them into Freddy's hand. Ravenwood stared at the night watchman. His shirt was blood soaked, his complexion ashen, and he looked as though he would pass out at any moment.

Freddy grinned back. "I know what you're thinking." He aimed his gun at Ravenwood.

Kolchak had stealthily come up from behind and now had the open end of his gun pressed against the back of the night watchman's skull. "Drop it!"

Freddy flinched.

"Drop it now!"

He dropped the gun.

"Now, give the tablets to the girl."

Freddy handed them over.

Shivering and clutching the tablets tightly against her body, she joined Ravenwood at his side.

"I might be a bohunk," said Kolchak, "but it looks like you're going to be a jailbird." He whipped out the pair of cuffs.

"I wasn't going to hurt anyone. Honest. I only wanted the money."

"You should have thought about that before you kidnapped Miss Whitfield and committed assault." He slipped a cuff around one of the night watchman's wrists. "Assaulting an old man and a civilian is bad enough, but you assaulted an officer of the law." Kolchak cinched the clasp. "A jury is not going to take that lightly." He grabbed Freddy's other wrist. "With all the other charges that I'm going to pile up against you, I wouldn't be surprised if you got thirty years."

Suddenly, the water began to bubble and roil in the reservoir—the surface glowed and an underwater craft broke the surface. Its exterior lighting filled the cavern with a bright glow, almost blinding.

Freddy shrank back against Kolchak. Eyes wide, he exclaimed, "What the hell is that?"

The dirigible-shaped craft was constructed from riveted plates that had lost their shine to a patina of mottled green and brown. The spiny rudder poked high above the stern, and in the center of the bow was a single, round observation window. Ravenwood deduced this was the sea monster the workers saw on the night of the earthquake. As sheets of water drained off the deck, the conning tower hatch popped open. A figure emerged.

Ravenwood recognized the face. It was the goon from the elevator the night he escorted Miss Whitfield back to the museum. His attire was different. He wore a long, flowing cape and a silver-skinned, widow's peak helmet that terminated between a pair of electric-blue eyes.

A rectangular port on the side of the ship opened. Hydraulic motors whined as a gangplank telescoped over the water. Inches from the bank it stopped. The man's approach terminated at the end of the walk, his galvanic stare fixed on the tablets snuggled against Miss Whitfield's bosom.

"Better give them to him," said Kolchak.

Darla raised her chin and defiantly shook her head.

"No," said Freddy. "I'm getting the million." He wrangled them out of her hands, the cuff swinging wildly from one wrist.

Without warning, Darla grabbed the tablets back from Freddy and slung them.

Freddy cried out as they landed in the reservoir with a splash. His face lit with rage as they quickly sank from sight. Impulsively, he shoved her.

"NO!" Ravenwood's cry mingled with her scream.

The ankle shackles abbreviated her steps, she lost balance, toppled, and plunged into the water. The links in the chain chattered like the rapid fire of a tommy gun as they swiftly slipped over the edge.

Ravenwood sprang forward, and made a desperate attempt to latch on, but missed. He dove in after her.

Red-faced, Kolchak extruded his words through gritted teeth. "I shoulda killed you." He grabbed Freddy by the collar and pulled him close. "You'd better pray that he saves her." The detective shoved him. The night watchman stumbled and sprawled across the walkway.

Ravenwood swam blindly down into the dark abyss. Even though she was bound by heavy chains, the swift current could have claimed her and deposited her in another location. He hit bottom and frantically groped around hoping she hadn't gone far. His depleting lungs began to ache. *Easy* he told himself. *Quiet your mind.* He remembered the teaching of the Nameless One. *Trust your feelings.* Ravenwood grew still. He let the things clouding his psyche slip away. In that second he felt the prickly fear of death shooting through the water like an electrical current. It came from behind. Ravenwood quickly flipped around and swam about ten feet before he bumped into her. He scooped her off the bottom and kicked his way toward the surface. His lungs were screaming for air. Finally, he broke the surface and gasped.

Kolchak was there at the edge to assist. He dragged her out of the water and laid her on her back. Her complexion was blue and she felt cold to the touch. "She's dead."

"No." Ravenwood crawled onto the walkway. "Place her on her stomach."

The detective rolled her over.

Quickly, Ravenwood straddled her and pressed the palms of his hands against her back and began to pump. On the tenth try, Miss Whitfield vomited water and gasped for air. He rolled her onto her back and sat her up. Even though she remained wild-eyed and continued to gasp for air he felt satisfied that she would be all right, and his mind was drawn to another concern, a blast of the Trumpet. His gaze was drawn to the deck. The Atlantean had the conch pressed to his lips and blew.

"Let's get the hell out of here." Kolchak hoisted Freddy to his feet.

The night watchman's eyes filled with terror. "LOOK!" He pointed. The water eddying through the subterranean canal suddenly defied all logic and the laws of physics. It immobilized and became as calm as a lake on a windless day. The blast of the horn increased by decibels and the surface rippled then jagged shards of water jumped up from the flat plane and danced chaotically.

Ravenwood felt his insides vibrating. His vision jumbled. "Run!" Ravenwood scooped Miss Whitfield up in his arms.

Single file, they hurried away. Freddy pulled up the rear. He let out a yelp.

Ravenwood looked back over his shoulder.

Freddy's flesh quivered. His scream was cut short by a loud *BOOM!* A second later, he exploded. His remains were no more than a thin sheet of goo running down the wall.

The synapses in Ravenwood's brain suddenly went awry. His bloodshot eyes bulged from their sockets. With his internal gyroscope gone, he faltered, knees buckled, and he went down. Upon impact, Miss Whitfield dislodged from his arms and rolled toward the water. It was all he could do to keep her from tumbling over the edge again.

"We're dead!" Kolchak cried and went down.

Voices filled the tunnel. One of them belonged to Stagg. Shots fired. The inspector's voice mixed with the melee of gunplay as he led the charge with a dozen law officers, armed with submachine guns, in his wake. The automatic weapons chattered, immediately followed by the report of sparks trailing across the dorsal of the submarine. Another spray of bullets struck the observation window. Cracks webbed out from the afflicted area.

BOOM!

A second later, two of Stagg's men exploded, and left an organic puddle of sticky mulch. The pitch of the Trumpet changed, lower this time. A violent shuddering seized the aqueduct and vibrated the stone-lined walls with ferocious velocity. Bricks shrieked as they exploded from their sockets of mortar and mud. A fissure spilt the ceiling and pieces of brick rained down. Stagg called for a retreat.

"We've got to get out of here!" Kolchak managed to get to his feet. He looked like a withered bloom that was about to drop from a dying vine.

Ravenwood took him by the arm.

"You can only help one." Kolchak shook loose. "Take Miss Whitfield and get the hell out of here."

As more brick rained down around them, Ravenwood hoisted Darla over his shoulder. They fled toward the nearest service entrance that led up to the street. On the verge of a seeming collapse the cavern shook and groaned, and despite the added burden of Miss Whitfield and the trouble of wobbly legs, Ravenwood made the climb.

The Next Day
Evening

Stagg sat at one end of the long dining table with a fork in one hand and a knife in the other. His napkin lay in a crumpled heap on his lap. "What are we having?"

"Patience, Inspector," Sterling announced as he entered the dining area pushing a serving cart. He stopped at the inspector's side and lifted the cover from the silver tureen.

"That's it? Soup?" Stagg huffed.

"It's the first course of a three course meal," replied Ravenwood.

Stagg looked relieved. He leaned over it and sniffed. He looked up at Sterling. "It's got a familiar odor."

"Odor?" The servant frowned. "I made this especially for you, Inspector. I heard of your fondness for peanuts."

"Peanut soup?" Stagg grimaced. "No thanks." He grabbed his napkin from his lap and surrendered it on top of his bowl. "I like my goobers dry roasted and lightly salted." He impetuously narrowed a cynical eye at the servant. "What's the second course?"

Exercising tolerance, Sterling replied, "Beef Wellington, sir, with a hot buttered diner roll, and steamed broccoli, garnished with chopped garlic."

Stagg smiled, then nodded his head. "That sounds more like it. I'll have some of that. Uh, but skip the broccoli. And give me an extra roll."

Sterling showed restraint. "Very good, sir. I shall have it out after I've attended to our other guests." He continued by serving Miss Whitfield and her father. The doorbell rang. "I'll attend to that." Sterling left. Moments later, he returned leading Kolchak into the room.

"You're late." Stagg announced.

"My car wouldn't start." He took the only vacant seat, across from Ravenwood and next to Miss Whitfield. "I had to take the bus."

"Better late than never," said Stagg. During the meal, the inspector ate a large portion of Beef Wellington and then had seconds. After he was done, he pushed away from the table, groaned, and clutched his belly. "I couldn't eat another bite if my life depended on it." Stagg's jovial mood disappeared. "Now, let's get down to business." He turned to Kolchak. "Give me the scoop because I've got newshounds wanting a story, and I've got the higher ups breathing down my neck, so, I'm going to need a prepared statement—PDQ—if I'm going to squash any rumors."

The detective remained quiet.

"There's a reasonable explanation for everything that happened," said Ravenwood.

"Okay, let's hear it."

"If you'll let me demonstrate," said the professor. "I think you'll understand."

The inspector acceded with a nod.

Whitfield stood, left the room, and returned shortly wheeling a serving cart. Beneath the white linen was a lump the size of a loaf of bread. He yanked the draping off.

Finally, Stagg narrowed his eyes and scowled. "What in blue blazes is that?"

"It's a harmonic cannon." It was square, made of wood, outfitted with two, trumpet-shaped car horns, and had several meters and knobs.

"Well, what does it do?" Stagg groused.

"With this machine I will be able to simulate how harmonics created the earthquakes." Stagg looked alarmed. The professor held up a finger. "Don't worry, it's on a much smaller scale." He flipped the toggle switch. Whitfield slowly turned the dial-o-meter. Both horns emitted a hum. The two, white, horizontal lines on the oscilloscope screen suddenly jumped up and danced in circles. With another tweak, the change of the pitch caused the dining table to shake. A few of the fine crystal glasses cried out and shattered.

Stagg jumped out of his chair. "Are you trying to kill us? Turn that thing off!"

Whitfield flipped the switch.

Everyone uncovered their ears.

Stagg flopped back down in his chair, picked up one of the glass shards, looked it over and tossed it.

The professor said, "Although the glasses appear alike, they each have properties that vary according to thickness, shape, temperature, and so on, and vibrate differently at the same sound frequency. That is why some shattered and the others didn't." The professor gave it some more thought then added, "And that explains why Freddy and some of your men—"

"Two," Stagg shot back. "Two of whom were fine family men and protectors of this city." He twined his fingers together. "You said this was a simulation, Professor."

"That's correct."

"What are you simulating?"

"The reservoir runs beneath the city like a labyrinth. If the wind were to blow across a fissure in the aqueduct it would become like a wind instrument and pipe the vibration throughout the city. Of course conditions like wind velocity and angle would have to be perfect to create this phenomenon."

"It would be like pressing a pop bottle to your lips and blowing," said Ravenwood.

"What's the odds of that happening?" Stagg asked.

"I'd say about a million to one," the professor replied.

The inspector didn't look won over. "What about the submarine? That wasn't the wind."

"In a way it was." The professor pulled out a wad of cotton from his coat pocket and stuffed a piece in each ear. He flipped the toggle up. "This is nineteen hertz." He gave the knob a twist.

Darla Whitfield was the first to succumb. She wavered. Ravenwood, Kolchak, and the inspector followed.

Moments passed before the professor turned the machine off. "If played long enough the sound will produce hallucinations."

The inspector knitted his eyebrows together and rubbed his chin. "I suppose the sea monster the work crew saw down in the aqueduct was a hallucination." Stagg shook off the last of the effects. "Yeah, but what about the earthquakes striking in isolated areas?"

"Quartz," the professor replied. "Where the soil contains higher concentrations of the crystal it acts as a sound receiver. If you spent the time and money for the resources to dig, I'm sure you would find crystals beneath the museum and downtown."

Stagg mulled it over for a minute. "Like a quartz radio."

Whitfield nodded.

"I don't pretend to understand all of this, Professor, but since you are a man of science I'll have to take your word for it." He nodded at the contraption. "Where'd you get that thing?"

"I have a colleague that works in the field of advanced sound technology. He loaned it to me for this demonstration."

Stagg stared at it before his gaze settled back on the professor. "Write a report on this and have it on my desk in the morning."

Whitfield nodded.

"I've got one more question. Why did the night watchman kidnap Miss Whitfield and take her down there in the first place?"

"Freddy worked at the museum long enough to know that a few of the displays in the safe are quite valuable. He held my daughter's life as collateral to force me to open the safe and take stone tablets that were recovered from a Greek temple. He tried to make his escape through the storm sewers."

Stagg pursed his lips together and gave a satisfied nod. He looked at his watch. "I've got some loose ends to tie up." He stood. "I'll let myself out." He got as far as the dining room door and stopped. He turned. "Hey, Ravenwood, I want you to show me where this fissure is. I'm going to have it repaired so this doesn't happen again."

Ravenwood knew a place where the aqueduct had caved in. He nodded.

Stagg left.

The sound of the front door closing reported back and Kolchak turned to Ravenwood. "I'm not in the habit of lying."

"Sometimes it's a necessary evil," Ravenwood replied.

"He's right," said the professor. "In this case, the truth would have been impossible to believe and the theories that I supplied are very plausible."

"There's still a blank spot," said Ravenwood. He eyed Kolchak. "What happened after we all evacuated the aqueduct?"

All eyes fell on the detective. He glanced over at Ravenwood's manservant.

"Alex," said Ravenwood. "Why don't you take the rest of the evening off."

"But, sir, who'll clear the dining table?"

"I'll take care of it." said Darla.

"Very well. I suppose I can take Miss Butterfield to a movie."

"Go on," said Ravenwood.

Sterling untied his apron, tossed it on the table, and left the room. Ravenwood got up and closed the door.

"Tell us what you saw," said the professor.

"I saw a merman."

"A what?" asked Miss Whitfield.

"Don't make me repeat it."

"But you must." Ravenwood retuned to his chair.

Kolchak heaved a sigh. "A giant merman rose up out of the water and wrapped his arms around the submarine and crushed it like it was a tin can. Then he dragged it under." He shrugged. "I—I know it sounds crazy."

"Maybe it's not so crazy," said Ravenwood.

"The Trumpet," said the professor. "What happened to it?"

"It fell into the water."

The professor's eyes sparked with hope. "The horn and the tablets could still be at the bottom of the canal."

"I doubt it," said the detective. "Something weird happened. The sound of the Trumpet stopped the water from flowing, but when it started flowing again it ripped through the tunnel like a tidal wave. I barely got out."

"I'm sure everything in its path was washed out to sea," said Ravenwood. "If the substation has been ripped from its mooring, the force of the moving wall of water will have carried away all evidence of the Atlanteans ever being there." The topic carried on a few hours until the fabric of the conversation wore thin. Ravenwood asked, "Would any of you like to join me for a brandy and cigar?"

"I'd really like that," Kolchak replied, "but I promised my boy that I'd take him to a movie. They're having a midnight showing of *Dracula's Daughter* down at the Bijou tonight." Kolchak shrugged. "What can I say?" The detective shook his head. "He likes that kinda stuff. Well, goodnight Ravenwood." He stuck out his hand.

Ravenwood shook it.

"Remember, if something like this comes up again and you need a partner." He pulled his hand free, placed his straw hat on top of his head, and gave it a pat. "Don't call me."

Whitfield approached, reached out, and clasped Ravenwood's hand. "I can't thank you enough for what you did for my daughter and the entire city." He shook it vigorously. Then the elderly Whitfield let go of his grip and grabbed hold of Kolchak's and shook it. "Too bad you'll both be unsung heroes."

"I was just doing my duty, Professor." The detective pulled free. "Sorry I can't stick around any longer and chat but I've got to go." He left.

"I'm afraid that I'll have to decline your offer as well," said the professor.

"Very well," said Ravenwood. "I'll see that Miss Whitfield gets safely home." He looked back over his shoulder. Darla was busy clearing the table.

After the room emptied, Ravenwood poured himself a brandy from the bar. He strode across the room to the windows to stare out at the lights across the city. A cigar and two drinks later, she strolled into the library.

"All done," she said.

"I'll get your wrap, Miss Whitfield."

"I think it's high time that you stop being so formal and call me Darla."

"Of course, Miss—Darla."

She smiled. It was alluring.

He was spellbound as she walked over to the bar, and helped herself to a cigar from the humidor.

Darla used the lighter on the silver tray to light it. She exhaled a cloud of gray smoke into the air. Next she poured a brandy from the fine, crystal decanter.

His chameleon eyes stayed on her as she crossed the room to the settee.

She sat and crossed her legs. The shift bared her shapely calves. "One more thing."

Still captivated, he watched as she reached down and unfastened the top button of her blouse.

"It's imperative that I live up to my promise to pay you for services rendered."

Now, Ravenwood was more than intrigued, he was mesmerized as she unfastened the second button.

Time: October 17, 1989 5:00 P.M.
Place: San Francisco Bay Area

David Combs strolled the sandy strip of the bay. It was a great day for a walk. Blue skies and warm, typical California weather. He was shirtless and barefoot.

At his side Sheree Tibbets waded the in the shallows. The wind strummed her long, blonde hair. She pushed it out of her blue eyes and pointed "Look." She didn't offer any further explanation, but waded out a little further, stooped, and dredged down into the sand. A moment later she held up a large conch. "This is a nice one." She kept her eyes on it as she rotated the shell.

"Let me see it."

She handed it over.

David finished his inspection at the spine end of the spiral. "It's a trumpet."

She laughed. "It looks like a shell to me."

"No, I'm serious. Look." He pointed to a small orifice at the tip of the apex. "The trumpeter blows into that."

"Show me." She tempted him with a smile.

He raised it to his lips.

The Moon Man

in

Mesmerized

by

Marlin Williams

Time: 1930s
Place: Great City

Fourteen floors up, Henry Thomas stood on the narrow ledge of the Frost Hotel. Terror filled his heart as he looked down onto the bone-crushing pavement. Across the street stood the clock tower. It was one minute until midnight, the hour he was going to jump. He didn't want to, but he couldn't help himself. A gust of wind whipped around the corner and almost ripped him off the ledge. His gaze flew back to the tower as the clock began to chime.

Nervously, he fumbled inside his coat pocket and pulled out a crumpled sheet of paper. He found a pencil in the same pocket and quickly scrawled across it. Another gust plucked it from his fingers and sailed it away into the night like a startled bird.

On the tenth stroke, Henry twisted around and quickly scribbled onto the wall. On the twelfth stroke, he turned back around and jumped.

Six hours later, Detective Stephen Thatcher was at the scene kneeling over the dead body. The hairs on the back of his neck suddenly bristled. He looked back over his shoulder and instantly felt annoyed.

"Another suicide," said Joe. The lanky officer took a bite of an apple and munched loudly.

"Maybe, maybe not." Stephen stood and looked around. "Where's your partner?"

Joe copped a smile that appeared half-cocky. "Jackson's talking to the dame at the register's desk."

The officer's stare went back to the body. "Just look at that suit. The stiff had money. He probably lost it in the stock market crash. He's just another fat cat to take a dive onto the sidewalk because they lost everything."

"I think there's more to the rash of suicides other than the stock market crash." Many of the suicides could be the result of the weak economy, but something was sending up red flags for Stephen.

Joe sniffed and thoughtfully asked, "Okay, so what's your take?" He stared at the detective, waiting for an answer.

Something else was going on in his city, something odd. Besides the multiple suicides, good, law-abiding citizens were claiming to be in a trance as they committed acts of crime. He had a gut feeling the two were linked, but at the moment, he didn't know what that link was. "I wish I knew," Stephen finally replied. He nodded at the pencil clutched in the dead man's hand. "We should look for a note."

Joe knelt down and began searching the man's jacket.

Stephen took a knee and removed the man's wallet, riffled through it, and found an ID. "Henry Thomas." The bill pocket held a small sum of cash and a few photographs. He placed the wallet back in the man's pocket and stood. He skipped a quick glance off the nearby surroundings. "Any witnesses?"

"The only person hanging around this morning is Mouse."

"Mouse?"

Joe nodded at the short, wiry-framed guy standing off to the side and fidgeting nervously. "He lives on the banks of the Upper East Side." Then he whispered, "Poorville." He raised his voice back to conversation level. "He comes down here sometimes and guilts the rich dames out of money. They got soft hearts for—" he lowered his voice again, "—the unfortunates."

"I wonder if he knows anything about Mister Thomas here?"

Joe shrugged. "Don't know. Mouse ain't much of a talker. Says so himself."

Stephen nodded. "I'll have a word with him."

"Good luck on that one."

He gave Joe a pat on the shoulder, and the officer went back to his search for a note and munching his apple. On his way over to Mouse, Stephen felt a tug on the back of his coat.

"Hey, Mister."

He stopped, turned, and looked down on the grimy little face staring up at him and instinctively felt through his hip pocket for a nickel.

"I seen somethin'."

"Oh yeah, what did you see?"

Immediately, the little boy looked down at the toes of his worn out sneakers.

The detective could tell that the words were on the edge of the kid's tongue, but didn't seem to want to roll off. "It's okay," said Stephen. "It's just you and me talking."

Slowly, the kid tilted his head up, but avoided eye contact. His expression looked strained like he was about to snitch on the bully who stole the milk money. "If I tell you, promise you won't laugh?"

"Promise," replied Stephen. He crossed his heart for good measure.

The kid looked away. "I seen Ole Mister Reaper." He squeezed his eyes shut and cringed like he was expecting the officer to slap him upside the head for saying something stupid like that. When it didn't happen, the boy cracked a lid. A bloodshot eye peeked through the narrow slit.

"Are you sure?"

The kid slowly raised his head like a turtle poking its head out of its shell and nodded. "He—was wearing a black robe with the hood over his head and he had this black box with blinking lights all over it." He looked at Stephen. "You believe me, doncha?"

"Sure kid, but where was he at?"

"He was standin' at the bottom of the clock tower just starin' up at that buildin' across the street. That's when I saw the guy jump."

"Do you have any idea when this happened?"

The kid nodded. "The stroke of midnight."

"Are you sure?"

The kid nodded again. "I heard the clock chime and saw the hands on the dial."

"Did you see or hear anything else?"

This time the boy shook his head. "Nothin'. I hunkered down and laid real still. I didn't want the Reaper comin' after me. I guess I just fell asleep, 'cause I woke up when the cops came."

"Where were you?"

"Over there." He aimed a grimy fingernail at the large field across the street overgrown with tall grass and weeds.

"Is that where you live?"

The kid nodded, "Sometimes." Then he looked frightened. "You're not gonna send me away to one of those work farms, are ya?"

"No." He let go of the nickel and fished a quarter out of his pocket. "What's your name?"

"Tommy."

"This is our little secret, Tommy" He handed the coin to the boy.

A king's fortune.

The kid broke out in a big grin. "Gee, Mister, a whole quarter?"

"I want you to take this twenty-five cents and go to the boarding house on Second and Plum. You know the place?"

The boy nodded.

"You give that coin to Missus Danvers. Tell her that Stephen Thatcher sent you. She'll see that you get something to eat and a place to sleep tonight. Got it?"

The boy nodded again.

"Good. I'll come by and see you. Okay?"

At first, the kid looked dazed. "Sure." Suddenly, a smile blazed across his face. "Gee, thanks, Mister."

"Get along then," Stephen told the boy.

The kid shoved the coin in his hip pocket, took off, and skipped down the street.

From the corner of his eye, Stephen noticed a wispy figure of a man. During his discussion with the boy, Mouse had crept in closer. The detective approached him and introduced himself with a warm smile he hoped would disarm any mistrust the vagrant might have.

Mouse nodded as a greeting.

"Did you see anything suspicious?"

Mouse said, "I already told that apple-munchin' flatfoot that I ain't talking."

Stephen reached inside his coat and pulled out a pack of gum, got one out for himself, and in a friendly gesture, extended the pack out to Mouse.

"Sure. Spearmint's my favorite." The little man withdrew a stick from the pack, carefully unwrapped it, plopped the gum in his mouth, and then proceeded to neatly fold the paper and foil into a small square. When he'd finished, he placed it in his breast pocket and gave it a pat.

"I hear you're from the Upper East Side."

Mouse nodded. "Yeah. So. What about it?"

"When I was a kid, I had a friend who lived there. Best pal a boy could ever have." Stephen thought he caught a hint of a smile, so he continued. "Guy's name was Frank Murdoch. Do you know him?"

Mouse turned his eyes up and to the right like he was thinking hard, then he lowered them and his gaze settled on Stephen's light blue eyes. Mouse nodded, and the faint smile brightened a little. "The guy with the glass eyeball?"

Stephen nodded.

"Yeah, I know him."

"Tell him Stephen Thatcher said hello."

Mouse shook his head. "Can't."

Out of curiosity, the detective cocked his head.

"He got himself outta here. Went to Hollywood and I hear he's doin' real good working for some agency." Mouse went silent.

He watched Mouse chomp on the gum several times before he spoke. "Look, I know why you come here." Mouse didn't react at all. Stephen continued. "Things are tough all over. Nobody is going to fault you for milking a few rich dames out of a handful of change." Suddenly, Mouse's demeanor changed, he relaxed a little, it showed on his face, especially in the eyes. "The way I look at it," said Stephen, "in some cases there's nothing wrong with the utilitarian approach."

Mouse stopped chomping and with a puzzled look on his face, eyed the detective from beneath a pair of knitted brows. "Huh?"

"Take from the greedy and give to the needy."

The bewildered look on the vagrant's face dissolved, and he broke out into a big grin. "Yeah. I like how you see things." His grin got bigger. "You know, Detective, you and me, we're a lot alike."

Stephen silently conceded, in that one way, they were. "So, as a pal, it would be a big help if you could tell me anything you know."

Mouse edged in a little closer, did a little rubbernecking before his gaze settled back on Stephen. "I didn't see anything other than finding the body this morning."

"Why didn't you tell Officer Joe this?"

"Heh, I don't like the guy. He's always tiptoeing like he's on eggshells around us homeless. But on the other hand, I don't think that you're that kinda guy." His smile broadened. "Are you?"

Stephen shook his head. "You don't have anything to worry about."

"Can I go now?"

"Sure," said Stephen. "If I need you, I know where to find you." As he watched the vagrant swagger away, a cruiser pulled up to the curb. The door opened and Lt. Gilbert McEwen stepped out and stood leaning against the car in a swirling cloud of cigar smoke.

Stephen walked over to him. "Good morning. What brings you out?"

"I've been cooped up in that office for too long." He'd had his lips clamped around his cigar, and it had made him sound like he had a mouthful of marbles. "I had to get out and stretch my legs." Gil nodded at the body. "What did you find out about the jumper?"

Stephen didn't like the idea that the department's head detective showed up so early in the investigation wanting information. "Just his name and where he's from. I'll give you a full report as soon as I can," he said, hoping Gill would leave.

"I think I'll stick around for awhile." Gil had twenty years experience on the force and had a real disdain for being shackled to a desk by paperwork. As the department's premier sleuth, and relentless man hunter, he preferred being on a case and matching wits with the city's bad guys. "What's his name?"

"Henry Thomas."

Gil yanked the cigar from his mouth. "What's happening with the citizens of Great City lately?"

Stephen shook his head. "According to the address on his license, Mister Thomas lived in Rockwell.

"Why would someone come to Great City to jump? Don't they have tall buildings in Rockwell?"

"I'm sure they do."

"Well then, it seems especially odd to me. Any witnesses?"

"Just one, so far. A boy about ten. He's a street urchin named Tommy."

"Okay, what did the kid see?"

Stephen sighed. "He claims he saw the Grim Reaper standing across the street holding some kind of gizmo with blinking lights on it while Thomas took a header."

"Oh, for chrisssakes! The Grim Reaper?"

"I'm sure with a little more questioning we can make sense of what the boy saw."

Gil looked like he was mulling it over. Finally, he broke the silence. "You said that the kid's homeless?"

"That's right."

Gil lowered an eyebrow. "You didn't let him get away without finding out where he hangs out, did you?"

Stephen bristled at the question, but didn't let it show. "Gil, you know me better than that. I gave him a quarter and sent him to Missus Danvers."

"I'll go by there and have a talk with him myself." Gil absentmindedly bit his lower lip as he nodded, then said, "Maybe I can get something relevant out of him."

As rough and tumble as Gil was, Stephen knew the department's head wouldn't handle the situation with kid gloves. In addition, if his interrogation became too calloused, Missus Danvers would probably whack him over the head with her broom. "Why don't you let me do that? I've already established a rapport with the kid. If someone else shows up to question him he just might clam up."

Gil looked as though he was thinking it over.

"The kid's pretty shy," Stephen added.

"All right. I'll let you handle the boy, but let me know when you find out something pertinent to the case." Gil turned to leave, took a few steps, and stopped. He turned around. "Do you think the Moon Man might have had something to do with this?" He pointed toward the body. The Lieutenant was obsessed with catching the Moon Man, the only criminal to ever elude him.

"Why do you ask that?"

"Think about it. The Moon Man wears a cape and that bubble helmet. Maybe that's what the kid saw."

"The Moon Man may be a thief, but he's not a killer."

"Capone didn't start out killing people either and look where his career took him." Gil took a drag off his cigar. The tip fired red. "Come to think of it, Capone's a Girl Scout compared to the Moon Man!" His words streamed out from his mouth encapsulated in puffs of smoke.

"He steals from the rich and gives it to the poor. What's wrong with that?"

"Ha! You're an officer of the law. You should know the answer to that!" He locked eyes with the detective.

Stephen let the heated statement hang in the air before replying. "I know you, Gil. You want to get to the bottom of what's happening in Great City as much as I do. So, instead of us knocking heads, we should be working together on this."

The frown on Gil's face faded.

"We're a team, you and I, and a good one."

Gil smiled, it was faint, but still a smile. "You're right." He slapped the detective on the shoulder and let it slip away.

"Then let me do my job."

"All right," Gil nodded. "I'll get out of your hair."

Stephen gave him an appreciative nod and the Lieutenant returned to his car and drove off.

Stephen walked over to where the little boy had said the cloaked figure had stood. Clues had a way of being in the open and invisible at the same time. You just had to know how to look for them. He found one. He stooped down, tweezed it gingerly between his index finger and thumb, and held it up for a closer look. It was a gum wrapper neatly folded into a square. He pulled a small paper bag from his pocket and dropped the evidence into it.

Joe sidled up next to him. He nodded at the bag. "What'd you find?"

"Mouse droppings."

"Huh?" Then he grew a big, clumsy smile. "Oh, I get it. What'd the Mouse have to say, anyway?"

"Mostly nothing. But I get the feeling he's a shady character."

"Speakin' of shady characters." Joe glanced back over his shoulder. "I've seen that Mookie character hanging around here lately." He frowned. "I don't trust that weasel."

Mookie Watts was kind of weasely. He just gave off that kind of vibe. About a decade ago, he'd been sucked into working for Tommy Gun Fleagle, the biggest crime lord in Chicago. Like most mobsters, Tommy Gun's crime syndicate bootlegged liquor and then laundered the money through the small businesses he owned. The Chicago police struggled to finger Fleagle with enough evidence to put him away until they'd caught Mookie on a separate grand larceny charge. Watts then snitched on the crime lord to get a lighter sentence. After Mookie did his time in the pen, the Chief of Police, Stephen's father, brought him to work on the force as a consultant. But, he was really hired to be the Chief's eyes and ears on the street.

"People change," Stephen replied.

"A zebra always has its stripes," said Joe.

"The term is; a zebra can't change its stripes."

"All I know is, once a grifter always a grifter."

Stephen watched a car pull up to the curb. Thankful for the chance to change the subject, he said, "Here's the crime scene photographer."

"It's about time. I put in a call over thirty minutes ago."

Stephen took the opportunity to head back across the street where the concrete kissed the grass. To get a sense of what the boy would have been able to see, he waded out to the trampled patch. At his feet was a makeshift bed of newspapers. One headline caught his eye, so he bent and scooped it from the ground. It read: **Nicholas Martini Slated To Run For Mayor After Visit To Washington DC.** Big Nick, as his close acquaintances referred to him, had opened soup kitchens all over the city and had provided good paying jobs to some of the locals. The word got around that Nicholas Martini was one of the good guys. *But you could bet that it isn't out of the goodness of his heart.* Big Nick's philanthropy made him a shoo-in against the city's incumbent mayor. With teeth gritted, he wadded the whole newspaper page into a tight ball and tossed it.

Stephen stalked past Joe and the photographer and entered the lobby of the Frost Hotel. On the other side of the lobby stood three phone booths, two of which were unoccupied. He entered one, closed the door, and made his first call to Maxie Corman, the reporter that had written the article on Nicholas Martini. Maxie confirmed the story was true, and then he divulged some information that wasn't mentioned in the article. Big Nick would be out of town today and tomorrow. This is what Stephen had hoped for. He thanked the man and hung up, deposited another dime, and dialed. A familiar voice answered. Five dimes later he hung up and stepped outside the booth. According to the clock on the wall, an hour had passed.

The concierge approached him with a pained looked on his face. "How much longer are you going to let that body lay in front of my hotel?"

"We have to wait for the coroner to pronounce him dead."

The concierge chuckled then huffed. "Any fool can tell you that the man is dead."

Stephen shrugged. "I still have to follow procedure."

The man frowned at the detective and said, "You do realize that Herbert Hoover and Jean Harlow have been guests at this establishment?"

"What are you getting at?"

"The Frost Hotel is an essential key to this city's commerce and I can't let our guests be disturbed by officers crawling the establishment like vermin." He planted his hands on his hips. "And, stepping over a dead body like a bad welcome mat."

"Okay, what would you have me do?" He capped the question with open hands.

"Hurry it up."

Stephen lowered his hands. "Sorry, fella, you can't hurry progress, as they say."

"The mayor has been our guest on several occasions, and I know him quite well. And I will call him if you don't speed things up." The concierge folded his arms across his chest and smirked.

Stephen had to give the man points for tenacity, but now he was beginning to get irritated. "Go ahead."

The man's smile folded in on itself and with a frown on his face, he narrowed his eyes at Stephen. "I can assure you, Detective, that I'm not making an idle threat."

"The mayor knows how the process works. If he doesn't tell you to take a flying leap out of one of your windows, then I will." The detective turned and marched away.

He returned to where the man had pancaked on the concrete. In his absence, the scene had been cleared. Only a bloody spot and a chalk outline remained. Something crunched beneath his foot. He lifted his shoe. On the sidewalk was a small heap of crushed glass and a bit of metal. A camera's flashbulb. Stephen was irritated by the photographer's apathetic sloppiness that left the scene contaminated. The detective knelt and did the best he could to gather up the pieces of the spent bulb into the palm of his hand.

"Hey, Detective," a male voice called out.

Stephen stood and whirled around. It was Joe's partner, Jackson, and he was solo and approaching quickly.

When the officer arrived, Stephen asked, "Where's Joe?"

"He went with the meat wagon."

This was good. Without the gangly officer, Joe, hanging around and jabbering away Stephen could concentrate.

"I found something," said Jackson. "It's a word. It could be foreign."

"Where?"

"Follow me," said Jackson, "and I'll show you."

They entered the Frost Hotel and as they crossed the lobby the concierge took the opportunity to glare at Stephen all the way to the elevator.

The photographer's up there," said Jackson as the grated door whisked closed. "He got a picture of it."

On the fourteenth floor, in room twelve, the photographer was busy taking pictures of the small cubicle and ejecting spent bulbs onto the floor. Stephen marched over to him, grabbed the man's hand.

With a bewildered look on his face, the photographer watched impassively as Stephen dumped renderings of the crushed glass into his open palm.

"Don't ever contaminate my crime scene again." He looked at the spent bulbs littering the floor. "And get these cleaned up."

"Over here." It was Jackson.

Stephen walked over to where the officer was hanging halfway out the window.

He pulled himself in. "Take a look for yourself."

The detective leaned out the window and saw the word. It was scribbled out in pencil. The dead man on the sidewalk had a pencil clutched in his hand. There was a good chance that he wrote the word before jumping. Stephen hoisted himself back inside.

"Can you pronounce it?"

Stephen nodded. "Sedgwick."

Jackson wrinkled his brow and scratched his head. "What ya suppose that means?"

Stephen shrugged. "Could be just about anything. Did you find any other clues?

Jackson shook his head. "Not yet."

"Let me know when you do."

"Where you going?"

"Back to my office to start a report." Stephen turned. The meek reporter had gathered the flashbulbs and stuffed the things in his hip pockets making them flair out like a pair of riding pants. He stepped back as Stephen passed.

It was on the drive back that he tried to process the morning's events and connect the dots, but one unrelated incident kept yammering at the back of his mind like a colicky baby until Stephen addressed it. The detective altered his course. He got within a block of Fast Eddie's Pool Hall and parked his car. The place served as a hub for every bruno, goon, hatchet man, torpedo, and triggerman for every crime syndicate in Great City. Inside the establishment, they were cohorts swapping stories of their latest sexual conquests, and sometimes, for the right price, beneficial information. On the street, they were enemies killing each other for control of territories and bootleg operations.

Stephen got out, and walked up to the door, opened it a crack, but didn't enter. Instead, he listened. Above the din of jumbled voices and other pool hall noise, Mookie Watts' voice carried. Stephen released the door and hurried around the corner to the alley where he shared the space with an unconscious rum head for close to an hour before he heard Mookie's voice outside the joint.

Without a moment's hesitation, Stephen whipped around the corner and plucked Watts from his circle of reprobates by the arm.

Mookie futilely tried digging his heels into the concrete. "Hey, Thatcher, what's this all about?"

The detective dragged the man to the curb and stopped. He figured that they were just shy of earshot of the other degenerates if they kept their voices down. He let go of Watts' arm. "I need some information."

"What?" Mookie shot a quick glance at the others. "Are you crazy, Thatcher?" He kept his voice low.

"I need to know what Big Nick's plans are once he gets into office."

Mookie smirked, chuckled. "I ain't got nothin' to say to you, Copper." The words from his mouth flowed out strong and loud. He chuckled again. "Arrest me if you want."

Stephen slipped an arm over Mookie's shoulder and faced them away from the onlookers. "I'm not going to arrest you, Watts. I'm going to give you a pat on the back and walk away from here smiling." That, or a witnessed handshake with any member of law enforcement, was as good as signing your own death warrant.

Mookie stiffened. "All right, Thatcher, what do you want to know?" he mumbled.

After Watts delivered the information, Stephen reared back his fist and slugged Mookie with a haymaker that sent him sprawling to the ground.

It took a minute before the man climbed his way out of a foggy mind and sat up. He wiped the trickle of blood at the corner of his mouth with the back of his hand and gave the detective a faint nod of appreciation.

Stephen turned and walked away. It wasn't until he passed the cluster of trouble-makers that they rushed over and helped Mookie to his feet. The detective got in his squad car and drove away, and when he pulled into to the precinct parking lot, Stephen sidled up next to Gil's car, got out, and waltzed through the double glass doors.

With a smile on his face, Desk Sergeant Mulcahy had his eyes locked on the young detective. "Sue called. She wants you to give her a ring as soon as possible." As Stephen walked past, Mulcahy gave him a wink.

Stephen breezed past the man without acknowledging his innuendo.

Hey," Mulcahy called after him. "Did you hear what I said?"

Stephen gave the man the OK sign and kept walking. When he entered his office, he grabbed the phonebook from his desk drawer, flipped through the pages, scanning the listings, and found none for Sedgwick. He left the book open and headed down the hall to McEwen's office.

Gil's door stood open. Stephen rapped his fist against the jamb as he entered.

The lieutenant detective was pressing the palms of his hands against the steel-gray panels of his hair like he was squeezing pain out of his head like a tube of toothpaste. He looked up from the mountain of paperwork sprawled across his desk. "Did you talk with the kid?"

"Not yet. Jackson found something pertinent."

"What?" Gil wrinkled his brow at the young detective.

"The cat that jumped from the Frost Hotel scribbled the word Sedgwick on the wall outside his window before he took a header." Stephen could see the gears turning inside the lieutenant's mind. Gil fired up his stogie. It was like watching a contraption fired by a wood-stoked boiler as the tendril of smoke curled from the end of the cigar.

"Sedgwick." McEwen folded his arms across his chest and settled back in his chair. "It could be a name. I'll check the listings." Gil happily pushed the paperwork aside and grabbed the phonebook.

Stephen shook his head. "I've already done that."

"Got any other ideas?"

"Maybe. But first I've got to make a call."

Stephen returned to his stuffy office, marched straight for the transom, and pulled it open. Instantly, a breeze streamed through the open hole carrying with it the smells and sounds of the city. He sat down and grabbed the candlestick phone. "Operator, get me Sue McEwen." The second hand on the wall clock made a sweep from the three to the six before she answered. Stephen said, "Hi, Doll." He leaned back in his chair, and with a grin on his face, replied to her offer for dinner. "Your place at six? Sure, Doll. I'll see you then." He cradled the receiver, and almost immediately, his mind went back to his conversation with Mookie. The same inner voice was yelling at him again, claiming everything that was happening was tied together. His hunches were seldom wrong. Stephen grabbed one of the files off the stack that contained the names of the recent jumpers. He delved into the dossier and lost track of time. It wasn't until Gil filled the frame of Stephen's office door and harrumphed that he surfaced from his meanderings and looked up.

Gil stood there scowling. His gaze switched to the file. "Has that got something to do with Sedgwick?"

Stephen felt it did. He didn't know how, not yet, but was operating on pure instinct. "It could be." Stephen closed the current file and tucked the stack away in a drawer.

Gil grumbled something about staying focused and disappeared.

Stephen returned to Gil's office, the rest of the day's time seemed to collapse in on itself as they did an exhaustive search for all venues that would lead them to Sedgwick. By five in the afternoon, they'd hit a dead end.

"This is going to be like finding a needle in a haystack." Gil settled back in his chair. "It's going to take longer than I thought."

Stephen looked at his watch. He suffered the pang of disappointment. He'd have to cancel his evening with Sue and the equally pleasant covert operation he'd planned for later that night.

Gil fidgeted and looked at his own watch, pursed his lips together, and with a rapid-fire motion, tapped his finger on the desktop. "We should call it a night."

This was out of character for Gil. Stephen probed the enigmatic proposal with a stare.

This made Gil fidget. "The mayor is not likely to approve of either one of us working overtime. We're already operating on a shoestring budget as it is. Go home, detective, and I'll see you bright and early in the morning."

The excuse sounded contrived, but Stephen left before McEwen did something like change his mind. The detective's sudden appearance in the foyer rattled Mulcahy out of a late-in-the-shift-stupor. The desk sergeant straightened his spine, and his dull eyes suddenly brimmed with curiosity. "Hey, Thatcher, what's your hurry? Gotta hot date or something?"

"Mind you own business, Mulcahy," Stephen lobbed the rebuke as he shot past.

At six, he showed up at Sue's apartment door with a box of candy and a bouquet of roses. He knocked, and the door opened. "Hey, Doll." He looked her over. "You sure are easy on the eyes."

With a big smile, she looked at the gifts. "Why, thank you, Stephen." As she threw her arms around him and gave him a kiss, the door across the hall opened a crack, and a pair of snooping eyes filled the gap followed by a harrumph.

He parted lips with hers and glanced back over his shoulder, and when Stephen twisted back around he was a little red faced. "Aren't you afraid of what your neighbor might think?"

She shook her head, "Nope," and pulled him inside.

The pleasant smell from the kitchen filled his nose. "Let me guess. Pot roast with potatoes and carrots."

"Your favorite," she replied.

He followed her in, plopped both the candy and the flowers onto the coffee table, and sat on the sofa.

"I'd better get water for the roses or they'll wilt." She went to the kitchen and returned with a crystal vase. She set it on the table next to the candy. While she arranged the roses, she hummed the song, *Cheek to Cheek* by Fred Astaire. When she finished, she stood back and admired them. "They're so lovely."

"Just like you," said Stephen. He picked up the box of matches sitting on the table and lit the candle.

She returned to the couch and sat next to him. The candlelight sparkled in her brown eyes. She scooted closer. "I just bought a new phonograph and I'm dying to try it out." She stood. "Let's dance the night away."

"I can't stay."

She looked disappointed and gave him a faux, pouty look. "But I need a dance partner." She stuck out her bottom lip a tad further.

"Sorry."

Sue tried again. "It's Fred Astaire's newest seventy-eight."

He shook his head.

The playful pout became real. "Ohhh, I may as well take it back to Sedgwick's and get my money back."

"What?"

Still wearing the pout, she replied, "I said I may as well get my money back."

"No, the other thing."

"What other thing?"

"You said that you bought the seventy-eight at Sedgwick's."

She nodded. "That's right. It's the name of the new place over on the corner of Fifth and Vine."

It made sense. The store had opened after the annual phone book had been published. Stephen jumped to his feet and headed toward the door.

She shot past him and barred it. "You're not going anywhere until I know what this is about."

"It's police business and doesn't concern you."

"If it cost me my dance partner and an evening with you, then yes, it does concern me." After Stephen explained the situation, she asked, "Are you coming back here after you visit the store?"

He shook his head. "Angel and I have a job to do tonight."

"A Moon Man job?"

He nodded.

Her sulky mood went away and she became elated. "Why didn't you tell me? I would have been prepared already."

When he saw the look in her eyes, he said, "You can't go this time."

"Why not?"

"It's too dangerous. We're hitting Big Nick Martini's place."

She looked at him for a moment and then began shaking her head. "You mustn't go there. Let's find another place to heist."

"This is not just about getting funds for the poor," he replied. Referencing the information that he'd gotten from Mookie earlier, he said, "I've heard through scuttlebutt on the street, that Big Nick is going to use that money to buy the election for the mayor's office and then put all of the cronies on his payroll in city offices. He'd have this city sewn up so tight that we'd never get it back."

"Even if Big Nick steals the election, his cronies would have to win their own elections first, and I'm sure the citizens aren't going to vote for them. Anything else and the people wouldn't stand for it."

"You've heard about the recent rash of suicide jumpers, haven't you?"

"Of course," Sue replied. "It's been front page news."

"I did some checking into it, and all of the suicides were huge donors to the incumbents' campaigns. The funds are drying up and some of the current office holders have already backed out of running for re-election."

"How would Big Nick force someone to commit suicide?" She looked worried. "Are you sure that's what's happening?"

Stephen nodded. "I know in my gut he's behind it all. That's why I have to stop Big Nick. Cleaning out his coffers would derail his plans and provide some relief to the downtrodden at the same time."

She stood up and folded her arms across her chest. "Stephen Thatcher, there's no way I'm going to let you do this without me."

They argued. They had dinner. They argued some more, and in the end he lost the battle when she retrieved a carryall bag from her bedroom and said, "Let's go."

"What's in there?" he asked.

"Things."

"What kind of things?"

"Girl things," she replied.

"Oh," he said, blushing, and thought it better to back off from the subject. "Let's get going."

It was almost seven by the time the detective cruised along Fifth with Sue at his side. The street was clogged with an army of lost and hungry souls parading the sidewalks that, for some odd reason, the depression hadn't slowed down. Maybe the Moon Man would soon acquire enough riches to alleviate some of their suffering.

He found Sedgwick's nestled between a haberdashery and a dry goods store. Stephen noticed one of the two windows on either side of the door was boarded over. He pulled to the curb. "You wait here."

The bell above the door announced his entrance. The walls to the left and right were lined with shelves stacked with miscellaneous electronic equipment. Down the center was a wooden display cabinet with phonograph records on both sides. Stephen walked past the albums to the back of the store. A man standing behind a glass case, stuffed with different brands of portable radios, stepped out from behind and glided over. He held out his hand. "Donald Sedgwick."

Stephen quickly scanned the guy before taking his hand and shaking it.

Donald Sedgwick thoughtfully placed a finger to his chin and looked like he was reading Stephen like one of those hokey clairvoyants in a tearoom. "You look like a cool cat. I'll bet you like Big Band and Swing."

Yeah, that was true, but so did most guys and gals his age. "I'm not here to purchase music, Mister Sedgwick." Stephen pulled his badge and held it out just long enough to flash it in the man's face before stuffing it back into the breast pocket of his jacket. "I'm Detective Sergeant Stephen Thatcher of the Great City Police Force."

The man lost his prize-winning salesman's grin and frowned. "Then why are you here? Have I done something wrong? Am I under arrest?"

The door on the back wall behind the counter swung open and a tall, attractive woman stepped out. The aquiline features of her face rested beneath the locks of long, black hair. With concern rooted on her face, she asked, "Under arrest? What for?" She took her place next to Donald.

"No one is under arrest, ma'am." Stephen pulled his badge once more and introduced himself to her.

"I'm Rhonda Sedgwick. What can we do for you, Detective?"

"I was hoping someone here could answer a few questions for me."

"Sure." Donald shrugged. "We don't have anything to hide." He chuckled.

"Is a man by the name of Henry Thomas one of your customers?"

The couple turned to each other, briefly held each other's gaze, and then shook their heads. Still shaking his, Donald turned back to Stephen. "No, we don't know anyone by that name. If he has any complaints about our merchandise—"

"No, nothing like that," said Stephen.

"What then?" Rhonda's expression was full of concern.

"He jumped from the Frost Hotel last night."

The woman balled her hand into a fist and shoved it against a tight-lipped grimace. She recovered from the shock and let her hand fall. "That's terrible." She shook her head.

"I don't understand," said Donald. "What has that got to do with us?"

"Mister Thomas scribbled the name Sedgwick on the side of the building before he jumped. And you folks appear to be the only ones in the city with that name."

"If he's a customer here, I would have his name in the receipt book." She hurried behind the counter and flipped through the pages. She looked up and shook her head. "I'm sorry, Detective, no one by that name."

"Do you have any relatives that live in the city or know anyone else that goes by the name of Sedgwick?"

They both shook their heads.

Stephen felt let down.

"Wait a minute." Rhonda thumbed back through the pages. "Neville Scorch!"

Stephen was puzzled. "Who is Neville Scorch?"

She opened her mouth to speak.

"Wait a minute." The detective fished a notepad and pencil out of his pocket. "Okay. Go ahead."

"Mister Scorch pawned a piece of electronic equipment here and said that a Mister Henry Thomas would pay the pawn ticket and pick it up."

"What kind of electronic equipment?"

"A black box with lights and a microphone." Donald scratched his head. "Odd looking thing." He stopped scratching. "I gave him a few bucks for it. I figured I could always use it for spare parts if no one came to claim it."

"May I see it?" Stephen looked around the room searching the shelves.

"It's not here." The tone in Rhonda's voice almost sounded apologetic.

"That's right." Donald nodded his head. "Somebody smashed the window and stole it."

"When did this occur?"

"A few months back."

He jotted down the information. "Did you call the police?"

Donald looked guilty. "No. It was the only thing missing. We were only out a few bucks. We have the person who pawns something sign a waiver against loss, so we weren't overly concerned."

"That's not the only reason detective." The contrite tune in Rhonda's voice changed to fright. "We were afraid of retribution. You understand, don't you?"

Unfortunately, he did. If a citizen ratted out a criminal that happened to be linked to a crime syndicate, payback was a sure bet. The detective nodded.

"What about Mister Scorch? Did you have any info on him like address or a phone number?"

Donald shook his head. "All we have is this receipt with his signature on it."

"Can you tell me what he looked like?"

"Yes," Donald replied. "He looked to be in his early sixties, white hair, and wore glasses."

"Height?"

"Maybe six feet," Donald held his hand a few inches above his head. "Average build."

"Anything unusual, like a scar?"

Donald lowered his hand and shook his head.

"There was something," said Rhonda. "He had a bit of an accent."

"That's right!" said Donald. "Sounded German."

"Anything else?"

The couple simultaneously shook their heads.

"You've been a big help," said Stephen. "If you think of anything else, you can give me a call at the precinct." The detective fished a card out of his wallet and laid it down on the counter. "That's my number at the office." He flipped the card over and grabbed a pen from the counter and scribbled another number down. "And that's my private number."

He watched Donald file it away in the drawer and Stephen left the store with at least something to go on.

He returned to the car where Sue anxiously waited.

Well?"

On the drive to his house he repeated what the couple told him. He pulled up in the long narrow drive at his place and stopped the car at the stone steps. The house was big. Sue was always quick to remind him that it was too big for just one person. Sometimes she'd say it as she wiggled her ring finger~*Hint~Hint*.

The front door opened. The artificial light spilled across the drive and a hulking figure of a man filled the frame.

Sue shoved her door open, jumped out, and raced to the man. She threw her arms around him. "Angel!" She gave him a kiss on the cheek. "How are you, handsome?"

"Ahhhh, Miss McEwen, I'm doin' alright," he replied, his voice deep and gravely. The big galoot blushed.

"You know," Sue said, "if I wasn't already taken….."

The giant blushed again. "Awwww, Miss McEwen, you wouldn't want to be seen in public with this ugly mug."

"Sure I would." She shoved the locks of misplaced hair back behind his cauliflower ears. She planted another kiss on his crooked nose.

The big guy shook his head. "You know I'm bad news, Miss Sue. You could get yourself into hot water being seen with me."

It was a well known fact that Ned "Angel" Dargan was the Moon Man's accomplice, and Stephen Thatcher, the detective, went to great lengths to keep his relationship with the ex-prizefighter a secret. "Okay, you two," said Stephen, "break it up." He got out of the car.

Sue pulled away from Angel and gave the detective a smug look. "Why Mister Thatcher, I think you're jealous."

He ignored her ribbing. "We've got some planning to do."

Angel turned around and walked back inside, Sue and Stephen filed in behind him. They walked into the study. Stephen took the chair behind the desk and the other two sat across from him. Angel's chair groaned a squeaky protest when he sat.

Stephen opened the drawer and fetched the rolled papers. He placed them on the desktop and proceeded to roll one out. "This is the layout of Big Nick's house." Angel and Sue gathered in as they went over the diagrams for two hours until they'd all felt satisfied that they had covered every possible angle and had left no holes open.

"Since Nick is out of town, all we've got to do is take out the guard and watch for any trigger-men still around." Stephen rolled the charts and stuffed them back inside the drawer. He stood. "Angel, you get the car while I get dressed."

Angel gave a nod and hurried out of the room.

After he was gone, Sue said, "I'll get your uniform." She left him and went upstairs.

Stephen closed his eyes and mentally rehearsed the plans again inside his head. He wanted to be sure that he had them down to a T. One slip and they'd be caught, or worse, they could die.

Sue returned and laid the cloak, gloves, and Argus helmet on the desk and silently left the room.

Stephen heard the door close. He opened his eyes, took a deep breath, and began to dress. He put on the cape and then the gloves. Lastly, he donned the helmet.

"You look quite frightening in that," she said as she came back into the room. The mirrored bubble distorted her reflection.

"You've seen me in it before."

"I guess I'll never really get used to it."

He removed it.

"One more thing." Sue got the holstered .45 automatic out of the drawer and strapped the belt around him.

Angel stepped inside the room. "I got the car, Boss."

"Good, let's go." With the helmet tucked under his arm, he led the way with Sue flanking him. The black, souped-up roadster sat in the driveway waiting for them, engine rumbling.

Sue climbed in and scooted across the bench seat to the middle. Stephen rode shotgun and planted the Argus helmet in his lap. It was a tight fit, but Angel managed to squeeze in behind the wheel. The back tires raised a ruckus when he stomped down on the gas, the car shot out of the drive and onto the street, and left a cloud of black smoke hanging in the air.

"Better slow it down," said Stephen. "You're going to draw unwanted attention."

"Sorry." Angel eased off the gas. "I've been looking forward to seeing Big Nick get his just rewards for so long, I'm anxious." Angel frowned. "You know, what he done to me and all."

Stephen knew what he was referring to. When Angel had been a contender for the World Champion Heavy Weight title, Big Nick tried to bribe him into taking a fall. When he'd refused, the thug had some of his men pay Angel a visit. They'd busted him up really bad, bad enough that it had ended his boxing career. He ended up on the street and destitute. It was Stephen that rescued the man from a living Hell, and for that, Ned Dargan was forever loyal.

Angel tightened his grip on the wheel and frowned. "It's payback time."

They cruised through the streets of Great City with the high-rises looking down on them. A full moon, hovering behind the buildings, tagged along. A good omen? Perhaps, thought Stephen.

Sue noticed it too, and pointed out that it looked ominous and expounded on her view that it would spoil the cover of darkness.

"We're in the neighborhood," said Angel. He gave the area a once over. "Classy joints."

Most of the estates were three story homes with rather large, well-manicured lawns.

Stephen pointed to the residence surrounded by a rock wall with flickering gas lamps riding the crests at graduated intervals. "That's Big Nick's place." Behind the wall, the gabled roof and spires poked toward the heavens.

"The place gives me the creeps." Angel stated. "It looks like Dracula's castle."

Sue was quick to point out the guard shack at the main gate. The guard himself was leaning against the wall enjoying a smoke. "This is where I come in."

Angel didn't slow as he drove on past. He went up a block, turned the corner, and brought the roadster to a stop next to the curb.

Sue climbed over Stephen and got out of the car. He picked up the Argus helmet from his lap and placed it over his head, walked to the corner and watched as Sue strutted down the sidewalk making a beeline for the guard.

When she was in front of the man, she stopped and hiked the hem of her dress way above her knee. "Ohhhhhh!"

Without taking his eyes off her leg, the guard pushed away from the wall and walked over to her. "What's the matter, Miss?"

"Just look at this." She nodded at her thigh. "I've got a run in my nylons."

He leaned in for a closer look then pursed his lips together. "It looks good to me."

To her, his choice of words sounded a bit wolfish, but that's what she was counting on. She rubbed her hand across the nylon. "I can feel it. See if you can."

At first, the guard looked taken aback, but then he grinned wide at the opportunity, reached out with his hand, and gingerly ran his finger up the seam. The moment the tip of his finger touched the hem of her skirt, she lashed out with a right hook.

The guard looked stunned, but quickly shook it off. His face contorted into rage. He wadded his hand into a fist and drew it back. "Why, I oughta—"

"I'll take over from here." Angel was standing on the sidewalk with balled fists.

The guard reached for the pistol in his holster.

Angel rushed him and the guard's gun clattered on the sidewalk. A second later, a melee of flying fists commenced; the guard catching the brunt of the punches. Angel launched a combination that rolled the guard's eyeballs back into his head and sent him sprawling onto the sidewalk.

"KO!" said Sue.

"Good to know I still got it," said Angel, smiling. He looked at his fists. "I remember the time I sent Max Baer kissing the canvas with these meat hooks."

Sue rubbed the fist that she'd planted the right hook on the guard's chin with.

"You're not so bad yourself," said Angel.

Stephen, now the Moon Man in full costume, walked up the sidewalk with two coils of rope, one slung over each shoulder. The one over the right had a quad-hook tied on the end of it. He approached the two pugilists and tossed the hook free coil to Angel. "Be sure you tie him up nice and tight."

Angel nodded. "Sure, Boss." The boxer turned and went to work on the guard starting at the man's feet.

The Moon Man turned to Sue. He ran his gloved hand along her cheek. "Good job, Doll."

She grabbed his hand and kissed it, and then looked up at him, catching the reflection of her face in the Argus helmet. With a well-practiced expression of allurement, she said, "So, does that mean I get to go along?"

"No." he shot back.

She went into pouty mode then anger flashed in her eyes. She raised her voice. "Why not?"

"Because the place is probably crawling with crooks, and crooks have guns. A good right hook is not going to stop a bullet."

She stared back defiantly. "Big Nick and his goons are out of town. You said so yourself."

"There might be a few of his thugs floating around here," he said. "If anything ever happened to you, I'd never forgive myself."

The look in her eyes softened. She nodded. "Okay, I don't want to, but I'll be a good girl and wait in the car." She was quick to hold up a finger. "But, just this once."

"All done, Boss," said Angel.

They both turned around.

The guard had been neatly wrapped from top to bottom with the rope.

"He looks like a mummy," said Sue. She chuckled.

"You said tie him up good," replied Angel.

"That I did," replied the Moon Man. "Drag him inside the shack so no one will see him.

With a nod, Angel obeyed.

After the guard was tucked out of sight, the Moon Man held out his hand to Sue.

She took it, and with sincerity on her face and in her eyes, she said, "Be safe. The both of you. You're two of my favorite guys." She turned and walked back to the car.

The Moon Man pulled the rope from his shoulder and played out some slack for the hook. "That should do it." He rocked it like a pendulum then turned to Angel. "Ready?"

"Ready as I'll ever be."

The Moon Man swung the hook until it arced out wide, then he let it fly. It flew over the wall and clattered. He pulled out the slack in the rope and the hook slipped up the wall and latched on the top outer lip. He held it taut then handed it over to Angel. "You first and I'll follow."

The big man took the rope into his meaty paws, leaned back, and scaled up the wall with the dexterity of a monkey climbing a tree. When he was at the top, he squatted; the moon was at his back making him look like an oversized gargoyle. He motioned to the Moon Man who ascended the wall with the agility of a well-toned athlete.

At the top, he squatted next to Angel, looped the rope around one of the pillar caps, and tossed the end into the yard. First, Angel went down. The Moon Man followed.

Meanwhile, Sue climbed into the seat, stripped off her clothes, and dug into the bag on the floorboard.

The light of the moon spilled across the lawn creating long, heavy shadows. The Moon Man and Angel crept stealthily across the turf occasionally finding refuge behind a clump of shrubs for reconnaissance. Stealthily, they made their way to the foundation's edge.

Luckily, the night was warm and the windows were open. Looking up, the Moon Man said, "The safe is on the third floor. But, we can get in here and move our way up once we're inside. Give me a boost."

Angel stooped and fashioned a stirrup with his hands.

The Moon Man planted a foot in it and Angel gave him a heave up to the window.

He parted the hanging sheers, crawled over the sill, and slipped down as softly as he could and stood in the living room. It was dark, except for the moonlight sifting through the curtains. A breeze rocked them gently back and forth.

Angel's face appeared in the window. He whispered, "The coast is clear?"

The place looked deserted. With a gesture of his hand, the Moon Man waved him to come inside.

Angel clumsily clambered through the opening and flopped down to the floor with a thud.

The Moon Man held his breath listening for hurried footsteps coming to check out the noise, but none came. He breathed again and chided the boxer to be more careful next time.

Angel nodded.

"Let's go," said the Moon Man, "and keep your eyes peeled and your ears open."

Beads of sweat formed on the boxer's brow and found their way down his cheek to drip on the floor as he followed.

The Moon Man pointed to the staircase.

Angel acknowledged with a silent nod and followed him to the steps. Cautiously, they planted one foot at a time and tiptoed up the stairs. When they reached the top, he motioned Angel to follow him down the long hallway. At the last door to the left, they stopped and the Moon Man grabbed the knob, gave it a twist, and with a noisy squeak of the hinges, the door parted from the jamb. With Angel at his back, the Moon Man crossed the threshold into the room. The safe was on the other side lit by a patch of moonlight. He was surprised to see the safe door slightly ajar. Maybe Big Nick was just a little overconfident. They made their way over to it and the Moon Man knelt down and pulled it open.

"Look at all that dough, would you," Angel exclaimed in a whisper of excitement. He opened the bag and held it out for the Moon Man to fill. Suddenly, there was a click and the room instantly filled with a bright, artificial glow.

"Well, well, look at what we got here," said Nick Martini as he swaggered into the room.

The Moon Man jumped to his feet and pulled the .45 from its holster.

Big Nick replied to the action with a cocky grin as a gang of pistol-packing goons filed in behind him. "Looky here boys, we got the infamous Moon Man."

The goons remained straight-faced and unwavering.

Big Nick nodded his head at the Moon Man. "Toss the heater or the big guy gets it."

He let the .45 slip out of his fingers.

"Now, kick it over to me."

The Moon Man sent the gun sliding across the floor with the nudge of his foot.

Big Nick picked it up and tucked it into the waistband of his slacks. "Apparently, you're not as wily as some believe you are. You swallowed it hook, line, and sinker." He turned to the thugs. "Get some rope and tie them up, boys."

One of the thugs nodded and exited out the door while the others kept the open bores of their guns trained on the duo.

Nick took a silver case out his coat pocket, opened it, loaded a cigarette between his fingers and shook it at the Moon Man. His grin broadened. "Then, I'm gonna remove the Moon Man's helmet and see who this cat really is."

"Are we gonna fit 'em both with a pair of concrete shoes and dump 'em in the East Bay?" asked one of the goons.

"Naw," answered Big Nick. "I've made other arrangements for the Moon Man."

The remark raised a few smiles and snickering while the others remained stone-faced.

When the opportunity arose, it was the straight-faced thugs that needed to be taken out first. The Moon Man glanced over at Angel and knew he was thinking the same thing.

Nick closed the cigarette case and shoved it back inside his pocket. "I almost didn't recognize you." He gave Angel a good once over. "Yeah, you've put on a little weight." He stuck the cigarette between his lips and lit it with a match. He blew gray smoke in the air. "If ya ask me," he said as the cigarette bobbed up and down, "Jackie was a putz for carrying you ten rounds." Big Nick started shuffling around throwing punches at an imaginary opponent. He stopped, took another drag of the smoke, and said with glee, "You shoulda taken that dive like I asked ya to do." He shrugged. "But then I woulda missed the pleasure of havin' my boys roughin' you up. Lucky for you, you lost that fight on the judge's decision, or else youda been fish food already." He snickered. "My boys kinda slowed down that right hook of yours, didn't they? A dislocated shoulder has the tendency to do that." He laughed again. "Now you're just a big palooka."

The thug returned with a coil of rope slung over his shoulder. "Here ya go, Boss."

Nick scowled. "Don't give it to me. Tie them up."

The goon turned to walk toward the Moon Man and Angel.

"Wait a minute," Big Nick called out.

The thug stopped and turned.

Nick pulled the .45 from his waistband and aimed it. The thug looked terrified and stepped out of the way just before Nick pulled the trigger.

An earsplitting blast filled the room and a spark flashed off the Moon Man's Argus helmet. It rang inside the headgear loud enough to make him flinch and leave his ears ringing.

Big Nick chuckled. "I guess it's true. That helmet is bulletproof." His expression steeled and he said, "Tie them up!" He tossed the .45 to the floor. "And I'm gonna give my pal, Gilbert McEwen a call." He walked over to the desk and snatched up the phone.

Before Stephen could react to the mention of Big Nick calling Gil, Sue stepped through the open door clutching Stephen's .38.

"Not so fast." She wagged the open bore of the handgun around.

Big Nick and the thugs spun around and stared at the women wearing a black, masquerade mask, a pair of tight pants, and a clingy, black, pullover shirt.

"Drop your guns," she demanded.

They all stood there mesmerized by the sight, everyone but Big Nick. "Well, whata ya mugs waitin' for, shoot her."

"But, Boss," replied one of the thugs, "she's a dame."

"Don't you think I can see that?" Big Nick cried out.

The thug lowered his gun.

"Shoot her," he commanded again.

One of the thugs wiped the stupefied look off his face and raised his gun.

The Moon Man sprang forward and knocked the weapon from his hand. Angel was right behind launching his own assault on the other goons. Within seconds, it turned into a brawl of hooks and jabs. Angel singled out Big Nick and caught him with a right hook that sent him flying backwards, crashing into a table, and left him lying limp on the floor.

Angel took a brief moment to say, "Washed up, am I?" He joined back in on the fight.

Between the two of them, Angel and the Moon Man wiped out the entire gang. They stood there breathing hard. Between breaths, the Moon Man asked Sue, "How did you get past the wall?"

"Yeah, the rope is on this side," said Angel.

She held up a ring of keys. "These were in the guard's shack and one of them fit the front gate."

Angel let out a laugh. "That's my girl."

Inside the Argus helmet, Stephen was frowning. "It was careless of you to come in here. You could have been injured, or—" He didn't want to think about it.

"Big Nick would have done something horrible to you and Angel if I hadn't stepped in," she replied.

"The funny thing about it," said the Moon Man, "is Big Nick was supposed to be out of town. Come to think of it, it was all too easy."

"Yeah," said Angel, "who stuffs a safe full of dough and then leaves the door open?"

One of the thugs groaned and stirred.

Angel asked, "What should we do with these thugs?"

The Moon Man nodded at the rope lying on the floor. "First we'll tie them up. Then I think we'll find enough evidence of bootlegging to put Big Nick and his cronies away for a long time."

"And don't forget about the loot," said Angel. "A lot of folks on the Upper East Side could use some of this money."

"And I know of a few charities that could put some of this cash to good use," said Sue.

After Big Nick and his triggermen were securely bound with the rope, the three scoured the house without finding a thing.

"Where could they be?" asked Sue.

The Moon Man looked around the study.

The other two watched with curiosity as he walked over to the ceiling high bookshelf and perused the titles.

Suddenly, he reached out and put his hand on one called *Gangster's Paradise*. He gave it a tug. The center bank of shelves opened to a dark room. As the Moon Man stepped inside, a small figure darted out of the darkness and pushed past him. Angel made a grab for the runner and managed to get a handful of shirt. The material ripped and the man scrambled out of the window shirtless.

The Moon Man raced over to it and peered out. The courtyard was empty. The Moon Man turned around. "Whoever it was is gone."

"It was Mookie," Angel replied. He still clutched the tattered shirt in his hand.

"Are you sure?" asked Sue.

Angel nodded. "I got a good look at the little fink."

"What do you suppose he's doing here?' Sue asked.

"The punk's working both sides." Angel ground out his words through gritted teeth. He turned to Stephen. "Your Pops should've known better than to trust a weasel like Mookie."

"Something's not right," said Sue. "We'd better get out of here."

"Not without those books," replied the Moon Man. He removed the electric torch inside the pocket of his cape. The beam revealed a cache of wooden file cabinets inside the secret room. "I'd be willing to bet this is where Big Nick keeps his records."

Angel stepped inside and found the switch on the wall. With the room now filled with light, they proceeded to smash locked drawers and dig out records of bootlegging.

Angel perused one of the books and held it up. "This is enough to put Big Nick away for a long time." He tossed it to the Moon Man, who put it on a stack with the others.

"Let's grab the loot and get out of here," said Angel.

"What about Big Nick and his men?" Sue asked.

"We make an anonymous phone call to Lieutenant McEwen after we leave here," replied Angel. "Him and his men will come in and—"

"What was that?" asked Sue.

"What was what?" Angel looked around the room.

"I thought I heard a car door close." Sue raced out into the study and over to the window. She pulled the drape back, then quickly shoved it back into place and spun around. A look of terror filled her eyes. "Boys, we've got company."

Both Angel and the Moon Man rushed over to the window and peeked through the gap in the curtains.

On the street sat four Great City police cruisers, the red cherry lights on top flashing red.

"What do we do?" asked Angel.

"Throw a smoke screen," the Moon Man replied.

Sue looked confused. "What do you suggest?"

"I'm going to draw their attention while you and Angel make a getaway with the cash."

Sue shook her head. "I'm not leaving you here to fend for yourself."

"Neither am I," said Angel.

"There's no time to argue, take the cash to my house. I'll meet you both there later." With that, he walked over to the window and climbed out onto the narrow ledge.

"Look!" one of the officers shouted while pointing up.

Almost immediately, a white light from one of the cruiser's hood-mounted searchlights washed over the Moon Man.

"Give yourself up!" The voice coming over the PA belonged to Lieutenant McEwen.

The Moon Man spotted a drainpipe. He edged over to it, grabbed hold, and began scaling it to the roof. The searchlight followed him. A shot rang out and a bullet struck next to him sending chips of stone flying through the air. He heard some of the pieces rattle against his helmet, but kept climbing. Another shot fired, this one hit closer. He grabbed hold of the eave and hoisted himself over the edge. As he did, numerous shots rang out, but he managed to escape the flying lead. Once on the roof, he stood. One of the bullets struck him. Luckily it was on the helmet.

He ran across the flat roof as a hail of lead flew by like a swarm of angry bees. Suddenly the firing ceased. He stopped to peer down and saw the Great City police officers spreading out to surround the place. If he was going to make his getaway, it had better be quick. He fled to the other side of the roof, looked down, and estimated the drop to be about twenty-five feet. But what choice did he have? He jumped.

When he hit the ground, he let his knees bend to absorb the impact and he went into a roll. He silently thanked a buddy that was a paratrooper who had once explained the method to him. He rolled to a stop and sprang to his feet. Now all he had to do was scale the rock wall, but the grappling hook and rope were on the side where the cruisers had parked. He quickly searched for another way out. There it was! A palm tree grew in a curved fashion within two feet of the wall. The Moon Man raced toward it and without breaking stride, ran up its trunk and leapt onto the top of the wall, and then immediately jumped off the other side.

He hit the pavement running. A light from behind spilled over him and projected his animated shadow onto the ground. He glanced back over his shoulder at the fast approaching headlights. He could hear the rumble of a car's engine. He stopped and turned and then pulled his .45 without plans of pulling the trigger unless—

The vehicle skidded to a stop in front of him. The beams blinded him. He tried shielding his eyes by placing his hand in front of the Argus helmet.

"Get in, Boss." It was Angel's voice.

The Moon Man let out a sigh of relief, raced to the passenger door, and jumped into the seat.

Sue threw her arms around him and gave him a hug.

Again, the back tires raised a ruckus as Angel stomped down on the gas, but this time, the Moon Man didn't reprimand his sidekick.

"We got the heat on our tail." Angel's eyes flicked between the rearview mirror and the road.

Stephen removed his helmet, pulled off the gloves, and wiggled out of his cape. He threw them on the floorboard and concealed them the best he could with his legs.

When he saw the red flashing light, Angel pulled to the curb.

Two cops popped out of the cruiser behind them brandishing pistols.

"Get out with your hands in the air," yelled one of the cops.

Stephen stepped out and held his hands high.

"Holy smokes," said the other cop. "It's Detective Thatcher!" He lowered his gun and the other cop followed suit. They both waltzed up to Stephen.

"Sorry," said the first cop. "We thought you was the Moon Man."

Stephen chuckled. "Me? The Moon Man?"

Sue waved. "Hello boys."

The second cop's jaw dropped. "Geeeeez, Miss Sue's with him too." He tipped his hat to her.

The first cop asked, "What are you doing out so late anyway?" He had a suspicious tone in his voice.

Stephen smiled back. "It was such a lovely night, full moon and all..." He looked up at the heavens.

The two cops looked up with him.

A few wispy clouds had gathered around the celestial body, and a few sparkling stars speckled the night sky.

They all lowered their heads at the same time.

As their eyes met, Stephen said, "We thought we would go for a midnight drive and enjoy the view and fresh air."

One of the cops nodded at the driver. "Who's that?"

Angel had his head turned away.

"A friend," Stephen replied.

The cop shined his light on the back of Angel's head. "Turn your face towards me."

Angel held perfectly still.

"What's the matter with him?" asked the cop. "Is he deaf of something?"

"Yes," Sue replied. "He can't hear a thing."

"Then what's he doing operating a motor vehicle?" asked the other cop.

A blast of static erupted from the two-way radio speaker and a tinny voice squawked out the call numbers of a squad car.

The other cop said, "That's us." He grabbed the second one by the shoulder tugged him around. "Come on!"

They scrambled back to their cruiser, got in and drove away with lights flashing and siren blaring.

"Whewwwwww! That was close," said Sue.

"Too close." Angel was looking a little pale.

"Let's get out of here while the getting's good," replied Stephen as he climbed back into the car.

Angel sped away.

As they drove back to Stephen's place, he started to fit the pieces of the puzzle together. He knew Gil was desperate to capture the Moon Man, so if he had to lower himself to be in cahoots with Big Nick to do it, so be it. "It all makes sense,"

With a wide-eyed stare, Sue nodded her head. "I saw Mookie in his office today. They were having a conversation, but when I walked in, Mookie clammed up and left like he was in a big hurry to get out of there."

"That's fishy," said Angel.

"It is," Stephen replied. "The whole thing was a setup. Big Nick made it public that he was going to be in Washington for two days hoping that the Moon Man would get wind of the news and take the bait. Then, when the citizens of Great City found out that he helped make the bust, it would be a feather in his cap when he ran for mayor."

Angel turned off the road and steered the roadster up the long driveway. Stephen got out of the car already feeling tired and stiff. He stooped and gave Sue a quick kiss.

She rubbed her cheek and frowned. "Hey, is that all I get for my troubles tonight?"

"It'll have to do," he replied. "I'll make it up to you."

"You'd better." She narrowed her eyes at him, but the smile betrayed her mock discontent.

He turned to the big guy. "Angel, would you mind driving Miss McEwen back to her place?"

"It'd be my pleasure."

Stephen watched Angel turn the car around and didn't set foot in the house until the roadster's taillights were out of sight. He bathed and crawled into bed feeling exhausted.

The wind up alarm clock on Stephen's nightstand went off at six in the morning just like it always had on the days he worked. This day was no different. He slapped the button and silenced the bell clanging in his ears. He yawned and sat up. Stiffness from last night's brawl and tumble had set in. "Owwwww!" He rubbed the back of his neck, got up, and on sore legs, staggered to the bathroom.

The phone rang.

He hobbled a quick step back to his bedside, caught it on the fifth ring, and pressed the handset to his ear. "Hello."

The person on the other end of the line sounded upset. It was Gil McEwen babbling something about the Moon Man.

"Slow down, Gil, let me get dressed and I'll be right there." He hung up the phone.

Thirty minutes later, he parked his car and walked into the Precinct station. Gil waited for him outside his office pacing the floor while puffing on his fat stogie. Small bursts of smoke were going up like smoke signals. Before Stephen could make his way over, Officer Joe strolled up. "Whoa!" he spouted. "Looks like the bed you got out of was on the wrong side."

Stephen huffed. "The saying is—"He huffed again. "Never mind."

"What happened?" asked Joe.

"Haven't you heard?" Stephen replied. "Curiosity killed the cat."

Joe chuckled like he got it. "That's a good one."

Gil looked irritated and stormed over to them. "Why don't you go play in the street while I have a word with the detective here."

Joe looked hurt. "Sure." He slinked away.

After Stephen felt the officer was out of earshot, he said, "You shouldn't be so hard on him."

"He'll get over it," Gil replied back. "Besides, I got something important to talk to you about. Just between you and me. Get in my office." He turned and stalked off.

"Sure." Gil's last statement shot a streak of fear through Stephen. He had a feeling that it might be something about last night, but he kept the apprehension from showing on his face.

The head of the detective bureau led the way as Stephen followed him in a trail of smoke. Once they were inside the office, Gil closed the door and plopped down in the wooden chair behind the desk. He swiveled it into a comfortable position and motioned for Stephen to sit in the chair across from him.

Stephen took a seat feeling like he was the suspect in an interrogation. He smiled. "What's on your mind?"

"I've got Big Nick and some of his goons behind bars at the city jail."

"That's great!"

"Well, it is and it isn't," the lieutenant grunted. "Big Nick said that the Moon Man and his sidekick showed up at his house last night ready to clean out his safe when a good looking broad," he used his hands to outline a curvy woman in the air, "hittin' on all six cylinders showed up with a heater and got the drop on them." He looked at Stephen quizzically. "Do you know anything about that?"

The young detective shook his head. "Why would I know anything about it?"

"Last night officers Flannigan and Smitty told me that they pulled you over in Big Nick's neighborhood. They said that Sue was with you."

"We were out for a ride last night. Anything wrong in that?"

Gil seemed to mull it over. He threw a couple of suspicious looks in Stephen's direction while he did so. Finally, he replied, "I guess not." He narrowed his eyes. "But what about the big galoot that was driving the car."

"A friend," replied Stephen.

His half truth seemed to appease Gil. The lieutenant pursed his lips together and nodded.

Stephen could tell that Gil was still thinking, so the detective nodded at the small stack of ledger books on the desk. "What's that?" he asked as if he didn't already know.

Gil snapped out of his thoughts and his gaze darted to the pile and settled there. "It's records of every barrel of hooch, every juice joint and barrel house Nick has supplied." He picked up one of the books and shook it. "There's enough in this one alone to put him away for life." He dropped it back onto the stack and picked up another one. "But this one has record of money that's coming from an unknown source." He laid the book down. "I'm going to find out where that money is coming from so that we can put an end to all of this."

"How'd you find the books?"

"The Moon Man left them in Big Nick's lap."

"Sounds like the Moon Man is one of the good guys?"

Gil's face reddened. ""He cleaned out Big Nick's safe, and in my book, anyone that steals is a crook."

Stephen settled back in his chair and prepared a question inside his head that had been gnawing at him since last night. "How did you know the Moon Man was going to hit Big Nick's place last night?"

"I didn't. It was a shot in the dark. I was hoping that the Moon Man would get wind of Big Nick's absence with that newspaper article and go for the loot. I planted Mookie inside the house to give me a ring if he did show up, and I was going to bust both him and Big Nick at the same time. Two birds with one stone." Gil's slightly haughty grin disintegrated and he glared. "One of these days I'm going to get my meat hooks on the Moon Man and then I'm going to put him in a cell. Right next to Big Nick Martini."

"Too bad he gave you the slip," said Stephen feigning a sympathetic look while mentally chiding himself for letting the Moon Man fall for the trap. He'd have to be more careful in the future.

"I'm close to nailing that clown," said Gil. "I can feel it in my bones."

Another thing that was needling Stephen was that none of his peers involved with the sting had so much as breathed a word about it. They had all remained tight-lipped about the operation. "So, why didn't I hear anything about this?"

"It was hush hush. I couldn't afford a leak. The ones I selected for the sting were sworn to secrecy."

That made sense, but the fact that he wasn't involved didn't. "So, why wasn't I invited to the party?"

"Well, I was trying to tell you yesterday, but you had your hands full with that jumper case. I don't want to spread you too thin. Your work would suffer and frankly, right now, I need your talent."

That made sense too. Stephen nodded.

Gil reached into his pocket and pulled out a small glass vial. He held it up and rattled the bottle.

"What is it?"

"A forty-five caliber. I found it on the ground outside Nick's place last night. The Moon Man must've dropped it."

This sent a new wave of chill through Stephen. He always kept reloads in his hip pocket. One must have fallen out last night when he jumped and performed the tuck and roll.

"I'm going to send it to the crime lab and have it dusted for fingerprints," said Gil.

Stephen quelled his fear with the fact that Gill would have to match it with a suspect, and his were not on file.

Gil smiled. "My first real link to finding out who the Moon Man really is." He looked down at the detective's holster. "You have a thirty-eight."

Stephen slapped his hand against the holster. "That's right, standard issue." He cocked his head to one side and squinted an eye. "You think I'm the Moon Man?"

Gil chuckled. "You? The Moon Man? No!"

It was hard to tell if Gil was being sarcastic or not.

"Have you got anything on that poor stiff that took a dive off the building?" Gil shoved the vial back into his pocket.

Suddenly, the precinct bells sounded.

A few seconds later Joe came busting through the door with a panicked look on his face. "The Great City Bank just got robbed!"

"Holy smokes!" The lieutenant jumped to his feet and pushed past Joe as he raced out the door. The young detective and the officer followed.

When they arrived at the bank, the sidewalk was already bustling with the curious and squad cars parked catawampus in the street with cherries flashing.

The trio pushed through the crowd and entered the building.

"What happened here?" Gil searched all of the occupants with his eyes.

An officer stepped forward. "Sir, these people said that they were abducted from their old folk's home and forced to rob the bank." The officer pointed to the row of men and women, clad in pajamas and robes, sitting in chairs lined against the wall.

The lieutenant stormed over to them and pointed a finger at an elderly gentleman. "You! What happened here?"

The man massaged his bald head. "I woke up this morning to a voice telling me to go outside."

The rest of the row nodded their heads in agreement.

"Voice? What voice?"

The man stopped rubbing his head and pointed to it. "The one inside here."

The row nodded again.

Gil scowled at the man. "If you ask me, it sounds like a bunch of baloney."

A portly man, with curly white hair and keen blue eyes stepped through the door and walked over to them. Officer Joe followed in his wake.

Stephen sensed his presence and turned around. "Dad!"

"Chief," said the lieutenant.

"Fill me in," said the chief.

"These scoundrels from the retirement home helped rob the bank and are blaming it on a voice inside their heads," Gil replied.

"It's true," said one of the women, her hair still in curlers. "I didn't want to go outside, but I couldn't help myself."

"That's right," said one of the others. "I couldn't resist either, and when I walked outside, there was a black armored car parked at the entrance."

"And a man in a black robe with the hood pulled over his head. At first I thought it was the Grim Reaper," said one of the women. "But he was holding some kind of box with blinking lights on it." She smiled, maybe at her prowess to recall the event. She nodded vibrantly. "Yes, it had blinking lights. I'm sure of it."

A little woman in a flowered robe raised her hand.

"Jeeeez," said Gil. He pointed to her. "You."

She lowered her hand, smiled, and said with a voice loaded with little school girl charm. "He was talking into a microphone."

Gil slapped his hand against his forehead and raked it down his face, and then he turned to the chief. "Somebody has been watching too much Buck Rogers."

A timid looking man said, "H-he m-made us g-get inside the armored c-car an-and drove us t-to the b-bank."

Another woman raised her hand.

Gil looked irritated. He pointed a finger at her. "Okay, you. What have you got?"

"He gave me a gun." She nodded once and looked proud.

"That's it?"

"Oh no," she replied. "He told me I was to shoot anybody that moved while the others loaded the loot into the back of the armored car."

"Then what happened?"

"He drove away."

"The first man that had been rubbing his head looked reminiscent. "After he was gone, I felt like I had woke up from a dream."

Gil scrunched up his face before he looked around the room. "Anybody got any aspirin?" After no one answered, he turned back to the chief. "Do you want me to book them?"

Little wrinkled faces stared back with eyes filled with anticipation.

The chief shook his head. "No. Make sure they get back to the home safely. I don't think they're going anywhere."

The little lady in the flower-printed robe raised her hand again.

Gil huffed and pointed his finger at her.

"Could we stop and get an ice cream cone?"

Stephen broke away to do a little snooping on his own. He scanned the room and every nook and cranny looking for a clue. He stumbled upon something lying on the floor. He stooped and picked it up. It was a gum wrapper neatly folded into a small square. He walked it over to his father and Gil and held it up. "I have something."

Joe looked at the tiny piece of evidence. "Well, there's the case cracker. Good job, Detective." He smirked.

Stephen ignored the officer. "I'm going to take a ride out to the Upper East Side." He shoved the wrapper into his hip pocket.

"We don't have time for a wild goose chase." Gil replied.

The chief held up his hand.

Gil frowned.

"Do you think you've got a solid lead?" asked the chief.

The young detective nodded.

The chief gave him the go ahead with a nod back.

The Upper East Side was a mass of crumbling buildings. In the latter part of the last century, the area was bustling with business and money until Big Nick's predecessor convinced the city's business council that it would be beneficial to move Great City west. Stephen was certain that it was either by threat or payoff. Without commerce, the East Side had spiraled into economic decay.

As Stephen cruised along the streets in the squad car, he gained suspicious stares from the destitute hanging out on the sidewalks. Even the children playing out on the hot, dirty streets watched him warily. He pulled over and addressed a not so friendly looking bunch through the open window. "Any of you know a guy that goes by the name of Mouse?"

Most shook their heads while the others stared impassively at the invader.

Then, one of the younger guys snickered. "That's just like the coppers. They only come down here when they need to make a pinch."

Finally, a portly, gray-haired woman spoke up. "I know Mouse. He's my boy." She planted her fists on her wide hips. "Is he in some kind of trouble or somethin'?"

"No, ma'am," Stephen replied back. "At least not yet."

His comment drew accusing glares as heads nodded and murmuring broke out in the crowd.

"Got any Jack...Dick?" interrupted the wise guy. He flashed a cocky grin.

The portly woman shoved him. "Lay off, Bimbo." She squinted her eyes at the detective. "Then, wha'choo want with him?"

"I just want to ask him a few questions," Stephen said. "About witnessing a possible suicide," he added.

The woman stared into his eyes like she was drilling down to the core of his soul; to the point where he felt uncomfortable. Finally, she nodded. "I suppose yer tellin' the truth." She nudged Bimbo. "Go to the blind pig and fetch up Mouse."

Stephen was surprised that she'd divulged his whereabouts using that term. Blind pigs were places where illegal alcohol was served, like a speakeasy. They had deceptive or blank fronts, often in basements, behind peep-holed doors, or in the back of legitimate businesses.

"Go on!" she said to the young guy.

He looked annoyed.

"You better git." She shooed him on his way with the sweep of her hand.

For thirty long minutes, Stephen waited in the car, baking under the sun, while the second hand on his wristwatch made slow sweeps around the dial. He felt thankful that the sidewalk dwellers had lost interest in him, at least for the moment. They went back to a casual conversation amongst themselves until Bimbo dawdled up the street with Mouse pulling up the rear. Stephen leaned over and opened the passenger door. "Get in."

Mouse looked wary. "Where we going?"

"You and I are just going to have a little chat."

Mouse looked at his mother.

She nodded.

He slipped into the passenger seat and closed the door.

"I've got my eyes on you," the mother called out. "You hear me?"

Stephen waved.

"So, what's this about?"

"Someone robbed the Great City Bank early this morning."

"What makes you think that I know anything?" asked Mouse.

The detective dug the folded gum wrapper from his pocket and presented it to him. "I found this at the bank."

Mouse suddenly looked coy.

"Cough it up, Mouse."

Mouse said nothing.

"We can either do this the easy way, or we can do it the hard way." Stephen unlatched the handcuffs dangling from his belt loop.

"Alright," said Mouse. He got a smug look on his face and suddenly reached out, snatched the keys, and ripped the microphone from the police radio. He then pushed the door open and bolted from the car. By the time Stephen got out, Mouse was racing down the sidewalk to where the land made a slight rise. Two taller buildings stood there. He scrambled though a small hole in the base of one of the walls.

Bimbo laughed. "You ain't gonna catch him now unless the Mouse wants you to." He laughed again.

Stephen ran to the dilapidated structures, knelt, and poked his head inside the hole. It was dark and the place smelled of urban decay. It was difficult, but he managed to squeeze his broad shoulders through the cavity.

Inside, a few shafts of light found their way through small holes and speckled the floor. He stood in the natural spotlight and suddenly felt vulnerable. Stephen stepped back into the darkness once again and listened for sound. The echo of dripping water clouded any peripheral noise.

"Mouse!" he called out and there was no response. The little guy might have already fled and was halfway across town by now, but that was speculation. He called out to Mouse again, and just as before, no answer. His eyes slowly adjusted to the gloom.

A shuffling sound snagged his attention and he caught movement out of the corner of his eye as someone quickly passed though one of the slivers of light. He pulled his .38.

To his right was a staircase. A ghostly outline of a small man raced to the top. Stephen pursued the phantom to a long hallway. The man was nowhere in sight. On one side, sunlight penetrated grime-coated windows. On the opposite wall were doors. He waded through the dust swimming in the air while the barrel of his gun led the way. He looked for a door that might be slightly ajar, spotted it, and stopped. He heard whispers.

As Stephen edged forward again, one of the floorboards sagged beneath his weight and let out a groan. The soft murmuring coming from the open door suddenly hushed.

His senses instantly heightened as he moved forward again and he applied a little more pressure to the trigger. The creaking floorboards continued to announce his approach. When he arrived at the door, Stephen placed his back to the wall and peeked in. Darkness stared back. He took a breath, yanked the door wide open and quickly stepped inside. The dim light from the hall followed him in. He saw faces, frightened faces. Two were childlike, and the other two, male and female, were older, worn, and worried. Stephen lowered his gun.

Suddenly, electronic static filled the inside of his head like the cold hiss of winter rain. A watery voice came through. *Shoot them.* As Stephen resisted the command, pain filled his head. *Shoot them.* Again, he resisted. His hand trembled and a red stream of blood trickled out of one nostril of his nose. The coppery taste of blood filled his mouth when it touched his lips. The voice repeated the command and he slowly raised his gun.

The father gathered both children into his arms. The mother took refuge behind him.

"Run," he croaked out the word, but the family remained frozen by terror. "Run, I said," his voice stronger this time and more commanding. "Get out of here!" said Stephen. He gritted his teeth and fought pulling the trigger. His psyche began to unravel.

A shot rang out.

Instantly, the voice inside his head disappeared, and so did the uncontrollable urge to pull the trigger. The shot had come from behind. Stephen twirled around. Gil stood at the top of the staircase holding a smoking gun. Between them stood a robe clad, hooded figure. The person held a black box with its electronic innards hanging out of the gaping hole created by Gil's .38. It fizzled and sparks rained down. The figure dropped the apparatus, tried to run past Gil, but the Lieutenant closedlined the mysterious person, and sent him to the floor.

Gil kneeled next to him while Stephen shook the last of the electronic fuzz out of his head.

Boy, was he glad to see Gil, for whatever reason he'd decided to tag along behind him.

The lieutenant pulled the hood back. "You know this mug?"

"Yeah." Stephen rubbed his eyes. "He goes by the name of Mouse." He walked over to the apparatus and picked it up.

"What is that thing?" asked Gil

"I think it's some kind of mind control gadget."

"Only one way to find out," said Gil. He reached down and patted Mouse on the cheek. "Wake up, Sleeping Beauty."

Mouse groaned and cracked an eyelid.

"You've got some explaining to do down at the precinct station."

While Gil helped Mouse to his feet, Stephen went to check on the family. He peered into the room through the open door. "You folks all right?"

The mother flinched at the sight of the detective's face.

"It's okay, I don't have a gun." Stephen held up his hands to show that they were empty. "See."

The father nodded.

"Look, I'm sorry." Stephen brought his hands down. "I couldn't help myself."

The woman, still huddled behind her husband, stepped out. "You got that Mouse?"

Stephen nodded.

"What about that machine?" the woman asked.

"Destroyed," replied Stephen.

They all seemed to relax.

Her worried look faded and mood brightened as she smiled. "Good."

"What do you know about it?" asked Stephen.

The woman walked to the middle of the room and pulled a string. Dingy light from a naked bulb filled the room. "Come inside." She beckoned him in with a gesture of her hand.

Stephen crossed the threshold and stepped into the room filled with shabby furnishings.

The father stooped and let the two kids slip out of his arms. He straightened up and looked the young detective in his blue eyes. "The Mouse used that contraption to make us all do things that we didn't want to do. Started out as small things like shoplifting and robbing local folks, but he was working on something bigger. He said if we told anybody, he'd put an end to us. We all agreed to keep our mouths shut."

Stephen mulled it over then nodded. "Do you know where Mouse got that gizmo?"

Both of them shook their heads.

Gil popped around the corner. "I've got Little Black Riding Hood shackled to the post rail."

They heard a loud crack.

By the time Stephen and Gil set foot in the hall, Mouse was fleeing down the stairs with his hands still cuffed behind his back. Part of the broken rail lay splintered on the floor.

Both Stephen and Gil pursued. They caught him at the bottom of the staircase.

Gil grabbed a handful of cloak. "You're not going anywhere, you little rat!" He jerked Mouse to a sudden stop. "Except to the cooler."

At Great City's precinct, both Gil and Stephen spent hours in the interrogation room with Mouse handcuffed to a chair. Exhausted, Stephen stepped out into the hallway where the chief was pacing under the green enamel shrouds of the ceiling lights.

"What did you find out?"

Stephen shook his head. "He won't crack."

"My concern is," said the chief, "There may be more than one of those devices."

Stephen had to agree that it could be a possibility.

The chief brought his hand up and clamped it down on his son's shoulder. "That's what you and the Lieutenant need to find out."

After the duo locked Mouse up inside a nice cozy cell, they hit the sidewalks and went back to the East Side. By late afternoon they had nothing new. Gil speculated that maybe the ones that did know something were afraid to speak up. Stephen had a gut feeling that he was right.

Mulcahy was behind the front desk when they entered the foyer. "No luck, huh?"

They both shook their heads and kept going.

"Wait a minute," said Mulcahy.

They both stopped and turned around.

"The chief wants to talk to the both of yous."

Stephen wrinkled his brow. "What about?"

Mulcahy shrugged. "Wish I knew, but I'm just passing the message along." The desk phone rang. Mulcahy grabbed it on the second ring. "Great City Police Department—"

They entered the hallway and stood in the chief's doorway.

Stephen recognized the look on his father's face as something serious was going down.

"Come into my office, boys," said the chief.

They stepped inside.

"Close the door," he said to Gil.

The detective lieutenant gave it a shove and it banged closed.

The chief sat down behind his desk.

"What's going on, Chief?" Gil asked.

"What I'm going to say is strictly off the books."

Both Gil and Stephen perked up.

"We're turning that gizmo over to the FBI," the chief replied.

"What's the G-Men have to do with this?" asked Gil.

"That gadget your little friend Mouse had was stolen from a German laboratory."

"What?" Gil looked stunned.

"That's right," said the chief. "We're going to hand that thing over nice and quiet to some German consulates, and no questions asked."

"I don't trust those Nazis," said Gil.

"Neither do I," the chief replied. "But we don't want to start a war, do we?"

They shook their heads.

"The thing that's puzzles me," said Stephen, "is how did the Germans know the device was here?"

"I reported the gadget to the FBI and the incidents that we knew were linked to it, and it seems that the boys from the SS were already talking to our government.

"And how'd Mouse know about the machine?" asked Stephen.

"There's only one way to find out," said Gil.

They hauled Mouse into the interrogation room and Stephen closed the door.

Mouse gave them a cocky grin.

Gil fumed, marched over to him, and leaned across the narrow table so that he could get in the little man's face. "Maybe you won't find it so funny when you're charged with espionage."

"Pftttt, yeah right, Copper."

"Seems that little contraption you had was stolen from a German military research facility."

Mouse folded his arms across his chest. "So."

"So," Gil replied. "That means that we'll turn you over to the German government for interrogation." Gil straightened up wearing a smug grin and said in his best German accent, "Ve have vays of making you tawk."

Stephen sat down in the chair across from Mouse. "Gestapo," he added. "And I don't think they'll give you the same hospitality as we do here at the Great City Precinct."

"I hear they use something called a thumb screw," Gil said to Stephen.

"Yeah, I hear it's a terrible torture device. They put your fingers inside a vise and screw it down until the fingers break or the fingertips split and spurts blood."

Mouse lost his arrogant grin.

"And that's one of the more humane techniques the Gestapo uses." Gil shook his head. "Too bad it has to be the hard way." He marched back over to the door and called for Joe. A few seconds later, the tall, thin officer was standing in the gap. Gil said, "Take this goon back to his cell."

"With pleasure," Joe squeezed through.

A look of terror came across Mouse's face as he held up his hands. "Wait a minute, fellas."

Gil placed a hand on the officer's chest. "Hold on a sec, Joe." He turned to Mouse. "You got something that you want to say?"

Mouse nodded.

Gil let his hand slip from the officer's chest. "Never mind, Joe, it looks like we won't be needing you after all."

Joe looked disappointed and nodded his head while giving Mouse the evil eye. "Okay, but I'll be outside in case you guys change your mind." He tossed the little guy another dirty look before swinging around and leaving the room.

After the door closed, Gil leaned across the desk again. "Okay, Mouse, spill the beans."

"Mookie told Big Nick that I had a contraption that would make people do what I commanded." The little man lost his tongue and diverted his gaze.

"Look at me," Stephen commanded.

Slowly, Mouse returned his gaze back to the detective sergeant.

"And?" Stephen prompted him with a glare.

"Big Nick invited me over to his place for a talk."

Stephen was sure that the invitation came by way several goons forcing Mouse into a car at gunpoint.

"Anyways," said Mouse, "Big Nick told me that he wanted me use the device to persuade a few of his adversaries to take dives off the rooftops of buildings."

"Why didn't you use the device on Big Nick?" Gil scrutinized the little guy through narrowed down eyelids.

At first, Mouse looked terrified by the prospect and then shook his head. "What do you think would of happened if it didn't work on Big Nick? He would have had his goons do me in right there on the spot."

Stephen nor Gil could argue the point.

"Then Big Nick had me rob banks and turn the money over to him."

Stephen turned to Gil. "I think you have your undisclosed source of money being funneled to Big Nick."

"Yeah, that and multiple murder raps I can put him and his goons away for a very long time." Gil eyed Mouse. "One more thing. How did you get a hold of that contraption?"

Mouse tightened his lips.

"Gestapo," Gil reminded him.

"All right, I'll tell."

"Hold it right there." He left the room and returned a few minutes later with a fountain pen and paper. He tossed them in Mouse's lap. "Write it down a detailed confession on how you got that machine and then sign it."

After Mouse scribbled out a written confession, he returned to his cell more than willingly as if the men from the Gestapo were going to appear at any moment and usher him away. He let out a sigh of relief as the iron-barred door slammed closed behind him, and he sank to the bed.

As they emerged from the hall and into the foyer, the desk sergeant's eyes were on them and brimming with curiosity.

"What is it fellas?"

They kept walking.

"What did the chief want?"

The desk phone rang. Mulcahy snatched it up. "Great City Police Department." He lowered the earpiece and didn't pay attention to the small, tinny voice on the other end.

Gil and Stephen were on their way out the door.

"Hey fellas, aren't you gonna let me in on it?"

They left the building leaving Mulcahy stewing in his own curiosity.

With a look of disappointment on his face, the desk sergeant returned to his call delivering a handful of uh huhs, and a sure, and a yes as he watched Gil and Stephen get into a squad car and drive away.

Twenty minutes later, they rolled up the street of a residential area and pulled to a stop in front of a white, wood-frame house guarded by a picket fence and garden of roses.

A distinguished man that appeared to be in his early sixties stepped out onto the porch and stared with curiosity as Stephen and Gill got out of the car. As they approached the gate the man struck a match off the porch handrail and stuck the flame to the pipe in his mouth. His hand trembled.

Stephen and Gil stopped outside the gate. Stephen broke the silence. "Mister Muller."

After sending a few puffs floating on the breeze, the man said. "I'm sorry, gentlemen, you're mistaken. His voice held a hint of German accent. 'My name is Scorch." He took a puff. "Neville Scorch." The man grinned. It was strained.

Stephen shook his head. "No sir, your name is Doctor Hans Muller. You're a German neurologist and you were a research scientist for Adolph Hitler."

The elderly gentleman suddenly looked nervous. "Who are you?"

Gil flashed his badge. "Lieutenant Gilbert McEwen with the Great City Police Force."

"And I'm Detective Stephen Thatcher. We have a man by the name of Alfred Douglas incarcerated at Great City Jail. He goes by the name of Mouse."

The man looked worried. "Come in." He looked past them like he was making sure no one else was lurking around. "Quickly."

They entered the gate, stepped up on the porch, and entered the home.

"The device?" Muller looked hopeful. "Do you have it?"

"What's left of it," Gil replied. "It got the short end of the stick when I had to rescue my partner from it."

Muller looked relieved. "Thank God."

"Do you want to tell us about it?" asked Gil.

Muller nodded. "The device disrupts the natural firing order of the brain's synapses. Once that occurs, the operator can manipulate the brain's neural network and the central nervous system will—"

"Whoa, Doc!" said Gil. "How about putting it in terms that me and my partner can understand."

Muller nodded. "The operator can hypnotize the subject or subjects to perform any deed, even if it's goes against the subject's moral codes and principles. And if the device is used over long periods of time, the subject's physiological brain structure becomes permanently altered. The Fuehrer used the device to hypnotize the people of Germany during his speeches. That's why I took it, along with all the plans, and left the country. I was to give it to a secret agent by the name of Henry Thomas."

Stephen's mind flashed back to the dead body on the sidewalk in front of the Frost Hotel. "Instead of handing it over to one of our guys, why didn't you just destroy the machine?"

"If I gave it to your scientists then maybe they could figure out a way to use the device to remove the hypnotic spell that the Fuehrer had placed on the citizens of the Fatherland."

"So, why'd you pawn it?" asked Stephen.

"For safe keeping," replied Muller, "I know the Gestapo is searching for me. I needed a place where the device would be well hidden."

"So how did Mouse get mixed up in all of this?" asked Stephen.

"I found him standing in one of the soup kitchen lines and hired him to do odd jobs around here. He must have overheard my phone conversations with Henry Thomas. The windows are always open." He took a handkerchief out of his breast pocket and dabbed the beads of sweat on his brow then stuffed the damp cloth back in its place. "Agent Thomas never showed up." He suddenly looked worried. "You must destroy the machine completely before it ends up in the wrong hands again."

Gil shook his head. "No can do, Doc, I'm sorry. The German government had informed the FBI about the machine and instructed them to return it immediately if found. Now they are sending consuls to pick it up."

Now, the man looked terrified. "You mustn't let them have it."

"It's out of our control. If we don't hand it over, it could start a war with Germany."

"If you do, Detective, I guarantee that the Fuehrer will be unstoppable."

"Well, the device is in pretty bad shape, maybe they won't be able to salvage it. And, they don't know that we've had this conversation with you or even that you're living here. But just to be safe, my suggestion is that you get out of here, pronto!"

"Like Argentina," Gil added.

Muller got a faraway look in his eyes. "Yes, I should go far away." He snapped out of it. "I'll destroy the design drawings, so even if they do find me, it won't do them any good."

After they completed the interview, the two officers bid him farewell. They returned to the Upper East Side and found the armored car hidden inside a derelict warehouse exactly where Mouse said it would be. All the money was still there and they returned it to the bank. The chief was particularly ecstatic. The city had suffered enough already, and this would alleviate a little of it.

There was one last thing to take care of. Stephen stopped by the boarding house and handed Mrs. Danvers a check for one-thousand dollars. That was enough money to house little Tommy for a few years and ensure that he got a good education. He spent some time tossing a baseball with the boy and then left the boardinghouse on the promise that he would stop by for visits regularly.

At the end of the long day, Stephen felt fatigued and looked forward to having the following day off. He returned to his house as the sun settled on the horizon, took a hot bath, and picked up his newest read, *The Case of the Counterfeit Eyes*. Three pages in, his eyelids drooped. The book went back on the nightstand and he turned out the light. Sleep came, with a series of bad dreams strung together.

When morning came, he woke to the smell of something good cooking. He knew it wasn't Angel making breakfast; his sidekick couldn't boil water without burning it. He clambered out of bed and slipped a robe over his pajamas and descended the stairs.

He stopped at the open door of the kitchen, and with a smile on his face, peered in. He watched Sue as she flipped pancakes and turned the bacon frying in a skillet.

She saw him and welcomed his presence with a smile. "Morning, Sleepyhead." She poured a cup of coffee and set it on the table in front of his chair.

He sat and sipped his coffee wondering where she'd found the ruffled apron she wore over her blue dress. She was humming softly to herself. A man could get used to this.

Angel broke the spell as he sauntered in and picked up the newspaper. "It says here that the German Zeppelin, the Hindenburg, is schedule to land here in Great City tomorrow before its scheduled rendezvous at the Naval Air Station at Lakehurst, New Jersey."

Sue came over to look at the front-page news. "Aren't those German consulates supposed to be on board that airship?"

"Yes," Stephen replied. "They're coming here to pick up that contraption."

"Good riddance," said Angel.

"Well," said Sue. "I hope that thing never makes it back to Germany. I think Adolph Hitler is a madman."

"That's my sentiments too, Miss McEwen," said Angel. "And anyone else who's involved with the German Reich."

"What about Doctor Muller?" asked Sue. "Father told me about your visit with him."

"That's a funny thing," answered Stephen. "After I left Missus Danvers, I dropped by to check on him, but he'd already cleared out and he must have left in a hurry because he left everything behind, including a note."

Curiosity surfaced in Sue's brown eyes. "What did it say?"

"It basically told us not to worry, that he had a plan that would take care of everything."

"Whadya suppose that means?" asked Angel.

"I wish I knew," said Stephen.

Angel shrugged and returned to reading the paper. His lips moved without sound.

"Let me see that!" Stephen snatched the newspaper from Angel and perused the article. "It also says that the Hindenburg is taking a large cache of gold back to Germany." He looked at his friends and grinned.

Angel said, "You must be thinking what I'm thinking."

"Yeah, the Moon Man's got a job to do."

The End

Printed in Great Britain
by Amazon

44116516R00101